Brought Home

Hesba Stretton

Table of Contents

Brought Home..1
    Hesba Stretton..1
    CHAPTER I. UPTON RECTORY...2
    CHAPTER II. ANN HOLLAND...5
    CHAPTER III. WHAT WAS HER DUTY?..10
    CHAPTER IV. A BABY'S GRAVE..15
    CHAPTER V. TOWN'S TALK..19
    CHAPTER VI. THE RECTOR'S RETURN..23
    CHAPTER VII. WORSE THAN DEAD..27
    CHAPTER VIII. HUSBAND AND WIFE...31
    CHAPTER IX. SAD DAYS..36
    CHAPTER X. A SIN AND A SHAME...38
    CHAPTER XI. LOST..43
    CHAPTER XII. A COLONIAL CURACY..44
    CHAPTER XIII. SELF−SACRIFICE...48
    CHAPTER XIV. FAREWELLS..52
    CHAPTER XV. IN DESPAIR...55
    CHAPTER XVI. A LONG VOYAGE...59
    CHAPTER XVII. ALMOST SHIPWRECKED.....................................61
    CHAPTER XVIII. SAVED..66

Brought Home

Hesba Stretton

Kessinger Publishing reprints thousands of hard-to-find books!

Visit us at http://www.kessinger.net

- CHAPTER I. UPTON RECTORY
- CHAPTER II. ANN HOLLAND
- CHAPTER III. WHAT WAS HER DUTY?
- CHAPTER IV. A BABY'S GRAVE
- CHAPTER V. TOWN'S TALK
- CHAPTER VI. THE RECTOR'S RETURN
- CHAPTER VII. WORSE THAN DEAD
- CHAPTER VIII. HUSBAND AND WIFE
- CHAPTER IX. SAD DAYS
- CHAPTER X. A SIN AND A SHAME
- CHAPTER XI. LOST
- CHAPTER XII. A COLONIAL CURACY
- CHAPTER XIII. SELF-SACRIFICE
- CHAPTER XIV. FAREWELLS
- CHAPTER XV. IN DESPAIR
- CHAPTER XVI. A LONG VOYAGE
- CHAPTER XVII. ALMOST SHIPWRECKED
- CHAPTER XVIII. SAVED

BROUGHT HOME.

BY

Brought Home

HESBA STRETTON.

CHAPTER I. UPTON RECTORY

So quiet is the small market town of Upton, that it is difficult to believe in the stir and din of London, which is little more than an hour's journey from it. It is the terminus of the single line of rails branching off from the main line eight miles away, and along it three trains only travel each way daily. The sleepy streets have old-fashioned houses straggling along each side, with trees growing amongst them; and here and there, down the roads leading into the the country, which are half street, half lane, green plots of daisied grass are still to be found, where there were once open fields that have left a little legacy to the birds and children of coming generations. Half the houses are still largely built of wood from the forest of olden times that has now disappeared; and ancient bow-windows jut out over the side causeways. Some of the old exclusive mansions continue to boast in a breastwork of stone pillars linked together by chains of iron, intended as a defence against impertinent intruders, but more often serving as safe swinging-places for the young children sent to play in the streets. Perhaps of all times of the year the little town looks its best on a sunny autumn morning, with its fine film of mist, when the chestnut leaves are golden, and slender threads of gossamer are floating in the air, and heavy dews, white as the hoar-frost, glisten in the sunshine. But at any season Upton seems a tranquil, peaceful, out-of-the-world spot, having no connection with busier and more wretched places.

There were not many real gentry, as the townsfolk called them, living near. A few retired Londoners, weary of the great city, and finding rents and living cheaper at Upton, had settled in trim villas, built beyond the boundaries of the town. But for the most part the population consisted of substantial trades-people and professional men, whose families had been represented there for several generations. As usual the society was broken up into very small cliques; no one household feeling itself exactly on the same social equality as another; even as far down as the laundresses and charwomen, who could tell whose husband or son had been before the justices, and which families had escaped that disgrace. The nearest approach to that equality and fraternity of which we all hear so much and see so little, was unfortunately to be found in the bar-parlor and billiard-room of the Upton Arms; but even this was lost as soon as the threshold was recrossed, and the boon-companions of the interior breathed the air of the outer world. There were several

Brought Home

religious sects of considerable strength, and of very decided antagonistic views; any one of whose members was always ready to give the reason of the special creed that was in him. So, what with a variety of domestic circumstances, and a diversity of religious opinions, it is not to be wondered at that the society of Upton was broken up into very small circles indeed.

There was one point, however, on which all the townspeople were united. There could be no doubt whatever as to the beauty of the old Norman church, lying just beyond the eastern boundary of the town; not mingling with its business, but standing in a solemn quiet of its own, as if to guard the repose of the sleepers under its shadow. The churchyard too, was beautiful, with its grand and dusky old yew-trees, spreading their broad sweeping branches like cedars, and with many a bright colored flower-bed lying amongst the dark green of the graves. The townspeople loved to stroll down to it in the twilight, with half-stirred idle thoughts of better things soothing away the worries and cares of the day. A narrow meadow of glebe-land separated the churchyard from the Rectory garden, a bank of flowers and turf sloping up to the house. Nowhere could a more pleasant, home-like dwelling be found, lightly covered with sweet-scented creeping plants, which climbed up to the highest gable, and flung down long sprays of blossom-laden branches to toss to and fro in the air. Many a weary, bedinned Londoner had felt heart-sick at the sight of its tranquillity and peace.

The people of Upton, great and small, conformist or nonconformist, were proud of their rector. It was no unusual sight for a dozen or more carriages from a distance to be seen waiting at the church door for the close of the service, not only on a Sunday morning, when custom demands the observance, but even in the afternoon, when public worship is usually left to servant-maids. There was not a seat to be had for love or money, either by gentle or simple, after the reading of the Psalms had begun. The Dissenters themselves were accustomed to attend church occasionally, with a half-guilty sense, not altogether unpleasant, of acting against their principles. But then the rector was always on friendly terms with them: and made no distinction, in distributing Christmas charities, between the poor old folks who went to church or to chapel, Or, as it was said regretfully, to no place at all. He had his failings; but the one point on which all Upton agreed was, that their church and rector were the best between that town and London.

It was a hard struggle with David Chantrey, this beloved rector of Upton, to resolve upon leaving his parish, though only for a time, when his physicians strenuously urged him to spend two winters, and the intervening summer, in Madeira. Very definitely they assured him that such an absence was his only chance of assuring a fair share of the ordinary term of human life. But it was a difficult thing to do, apart from the hardness of the struggle; and the difficulty just verged upon an impossibility. The living was not a rich one, its whole income being a little under L400 a year. Now, when he had provided a salary for the curate who must take his duty, and decided upon the smallest sum necessary for his own expenses, the remainder, in whatever way the sum was worked, was clearly quite insufficient for the maintenance of his young wife and child. They could not go with him; that was impossible. But how were they to live whilst he was away? No doubt, if his difficulty had been known, there were many wealthy people among his friends who would gladly have removed it; but not one of them even guessed at it. Was not Mrs. Bolton, the widow of the late archdeacon, and the richest woman in Upton, own aunt to the rector, David Chantrey?

Next to Mr. Chantrey himself, Mrs. Bolton was the most eminent personage in Upton. She had settled there upon the archdeacon's death, which happened immediately after he had obtained the living for his wife's favorite nephew. For some years she had been the only lady connected with the rector, and had acted as his female representative. There was neither mansion nor cottage which she had not visited. The high were her associates; the low her proteges, for whose souls she labored. She was at the head of all charitable agencies and benevolent societies. Nothing could be set on foot in Upton under any other patronage. She was active, untiring, and not very susceptible. So early and so completely had she obtained the little sovereignty she had assumed, that when the rightful queen came there was no room for her. The rector's wife was only known as a pretty and pleasant−spoken young lady, who left all the parish affairs in Mrs. Bolton's hands.

It is not to be wondered at, then, that no one guessed at David Chantrey's difficulty, though everybody knew the exact amount of his income. Neither he nor his wife hinted at it. Sophy Chantrey would have freely given the world, had it been hers, to accompany her husband; but there was no chance of that. A friend was going out on the same doleful search for health; and the two were to take charge of each other. But how to live at all while David was away? She urged that she could manage very well on seventy or eighty pounds a year, if she and her boy went to some cheap lodgings in a strange neighborhood, where nobody knew them; but her husband would not listen to such a plan. The worry and fret of his brain had grown almost to fever−height, when his aunt made a proposal, which he accepted in impatient haste. This was that Sophy should make her home at

Bolton Villa for the full time of his absence; on condition that Charlie, a boy of seven years old, full of life and spirits, should be sent to school for the same term.

Sophy rebelled for a little while, but in vain. In thinking of the eighteen long and dreary months her husband would be away, she had counted upon having the consolation of her child's companionship. But no other scheme presented itself; and she felt the sacrifice must be made for David's sake. A suitable school was found for Charlie; and he was placed in it a day or two before she had to journey down to Southampton with her husband. No soul on deck that day was more sorrowful than hers. David's hollow cheeks, and thin, stooping frame, and the feeble hand that clasped hers till the last moment, made the hope of ever seeing him again seem a mad folly. Her sick heart refused to be comforted. He was sanguine, and spoke almost gayly of his return; but she was filled with anguish. A strong persuasion seized upon her that she should see his face no more; and when the bitter moment of parting was over, she travelled back alone, heart-stricken and crushed in spirit, to her new home under Mrs. Bolton's roof.

CHAPTER II. ANN HOLLAND

Bolton Villa was not more than a stone's throw from the rectory and the church. Sophy could hear the same shrieks of the martins wheeling about the tower, and the same wintry chant of the robins amid the ivy creeping up it. The familiar striking of the church clock and the chime of the bells rang alike through the windows of both houses. But there was no sound of her husband's voice and no merry shout of Charlie's, and the difference was appalling to her. She could not endure it.

Mrs. Bolton was exceedingly proud of her villa. It had been bought expressly to please her by the late archdeacon, and altered under her own superintendence. Her tastes and wishes had been studied throughout. The interior was something like a diary of her life. The broad oak staircase was decorated with flags and banners from all the countries she had travelled through; souvenirs labelled with the names of every town she had visited, and the date of that event, lay scattered about. The entrance-hall, darkened by the heavy banners on the staircase, was a museum of curiosities collected by herself. The corners and niches were filled with plaster casts of famous statuary, which were supposed to look as fine as their marble originals in the gloom surrounding them. Every room was crowded with ornaments and knick-knacks, all of which had some association with herself. Even those apartments not seen by guests were no less encumbered with mementoes that had been discarded from time to time in favor of newer treasures. Mrs. Bolton never dared to change her servants, and it cannot be wondered at, that while offering a home to her nephew's wife, she could not extend her invitation to a mischievous boy of seven.

But however interesting Bolton Villa might be to its mistress, it was not altogether a home favorable for the recovery of a bowed-down spirit, though Mrs. Bolton could not understand why Sophy, surrounded with so many blessings and with so much to be thankful for, should fall into a low, nervous fever shortly after she had parted with her husband and child. The house was quiet, fearfully quiet to Sophy. There was a depressing hush about it altogether different from the cheerful tranquillity of her own home. Very few visitors broke through its monotony, for Mrs. Bolton's social pinnacle was too high above her immediate neighbors for them to climb up to it; whilst those whose station was somewhat on a level with hers lived too faraway, or were too young and frivolous for friendly intercourse. There were formal dinner-parties at stated intervals, and occasionally a neighboring clergyman to be entertained. But these came few and far between, and Sophy Chantrey found herself very much alone amid the banners and souvenirs that banished her boy from the house.

Mrs. Bolton herself was very often away. There was always something to be done in the parish which should by right have been Sophy's work, but her aunt had always discouraged any interference and David had been quite content to keep her to himself, as there was so able a substitute for her in the ordinary duties of a clergyman's wife. She had made but few acquaintances, and it was generally understood that Mrs. Chantrey was quite a cipher. No one ever expected her to become prominent in Upton.

About half-way down the High street of Upton stood a small old-fashioned saddler's shop, the door of which was divided across the middle, so as to form two parts, the upper one always thrown open. Above the doorway, under a low-gabled roof, hung a cracked and mouldering sign-board, bearing the words "Ann Holland, Saddler." All the letters were faded, yet a keen eye might detect that the name "Ann" was more distinct than the others, as if painted at a later date. Within the shop an old journeyman was always to be seen, busy at his trade, and taking no heed of any customer coming in, unless the ringing of a bell on the lower half of the door remained unnoticed, when he would shamble away to call his mistress. In an evening after the twilight had set in, and it was too dark for her own ornamental stitching of the saddlery. Ann Holland was often to be found leaning

Brought Home

over the half-door of her shop, and ready to exchange a friendly good-night, or a more lengthy conversation, with her townsfolk as they passed to and fro. She was a rosy, cheery-looking woman, still under fifty, with a pleasant voice and a friendly word for every one, and it was well known that she had refused several offers of marriage, some of them very eligible for a person of her station. There was not one of the townspeople she had not known from their earliest appearance in Upton, and she had the pedigree of all the families, high and low, at her finger-ends. New-comers she could only tolerate until they had lived respectably and paid their debts punctually for a good number of years. She had a kindly love of gossip, a simple real interest in the fortunes of all about her. There was little else for her to think of, for books and newspapers came seldom in her way, and were often far above her comprehension when they did, Upton news that would bring tears to her eyes or a laugh to her lips was the food her mind lived upon. Ann Holland was almost as general a favorite as the rector himself.

It was some months after David Chantrey had gone to Madeira that Ann Holland was lingering late one evening over her door, watching the little street subside into the quietness of night. The wife of one of her best customers was passing by, and stopped to speak to her.

"Have you happened to hear any talk of Mrs. Chantrey?" she asked. Her voice fell into a low and mysterious tone, and she glanced up and down the street lest any one should chance to be within hearing. Ann Holland quickly guessed there was something important to be told, and she opened the half door to her neighbor.

"Come in, Mrs. Brown," she said; "Richard's not at home yet."

She led the way into the room behind the shop, as pleasant a place as any in all Upton, except for the scent of the leather, which she had grown so used to that its absence would have seemed a loss. It was a kitchen spotlessly clean, with an old-fashioned polished dresser and shelves above it filled with pewter plates and dishes, upon which every gleam of firelight twinkled. A tall mahogany clock, with its head against the ceiling, and the round, good-humored face of a full moon beaming above its dial-plate, stood in one corner; while in the opposite one there was a corner cupboard with glass doors, filled with antique china cups and tea-pots, and a Chinese mandarin that never ceased to roll its head to and fro helplessly. Bean-pots of flowers, as Ann Holland called them, covered the broad window-sill; and a screen, adorned with fragments of old ballads, and with newspaper announcements of births, deaths, and marriages among Upton people, was drawn across the outer door, which opened into a little garden at the back of the house. There was a miniature parlor behind the kitchen, filled with furniture worked in tent stitch by Ann Holland's mother, and carefully covered with white dimity; but it was only entered on most important occasions. Even Mr. Chantrey had never yet been invited into it; for any event short of a solemn crisis the kitchen was considered good enough.

"You haven't heard anything of Mrs, Chantrey, then?" repeated Mrs. Brown, still in low and important tones, as she seated herself in a three–cornered chair, a seat of honor rather than of ease, as one could not get a comfortable position without sitting sideways.

"No, nothing," answered. Ann Holland; "nothing bad about Mr. Chantrey, I hope. Have they had any bad news of him?"

Mrs. Brown was first cousin to Mrs. Bolton's butler, and was naturally regarded as an oracle with regard to all that went on at Bolton Villa.

"Oh no, he's all right: not him, but her," she answered, almost in a whisper; "I can't say for certain it's true, for Cousin James purses up his mouth ever so when it's spoken, of; but cook swears to it, and he doesn't deny it, you know. I shouldn't like it to go any farther; but I can depend on yon, Miss Holland. A trusted woman like you must be choked up with secrets, I'm sure. I often and often say, Ann Holland knows some things, and could tell them, too, if she'd only open her lips."

"You're right, Mrs. Brown," said Ann Holland, with a gratified smile; "you may trust me with any secret."

"Well, then, they say," continued Mrs, Brown, "that Mrs. Chantrey takes more than is good for her. She's getting fond of it, you know; anything that'll excite her; and ladies, can get all sorts of things, worse for them a dozen times than what poor folks take. They say she doesn't know what she's saying often."

"Dear, dear!" cried Ann Holland, in a sorrowful voice; "it can't be true, and Mr. Chantrey away! She's such a sweet pleasant–spoken young lady; I could never think it of her. He brought her here the very first week after they came to Upton, and she sat in that very chair you're set on, Mrs. Brown, and I thought her the prettiest picture I'd seen for many a year; and so did he, I'm sure. It can't be true, and him such a good man, and such a preacher as he is, with all the gentry round coming in their carriages to church."

"Well, it mayn't be true," answered Mrs. Brown, slowly, as if the arguments used by Ann Holland were almost weighty enough to outbalance the cook's evidence; "I hope it isn't true, I'm sure. But they say at Bolton Villa it's a awful lonely life she do lead without Master Charlie, and Mrs. Bolton away so much. It 'ud give me the horrors, I know, to live in that house with all those white plaster men and women as big as life, standing everywhere about staring at you with blind eyes. I should want something to keep up my spirits. But I'm sure nobody could be sorrier than me if it turned out to be true."

"Sorry!" exclaimed Ann Holland, "why, I'd cut my right hand off to prevent it being true. No words can tell how good Mr. Chantrey's been to me. Everybody knows what my poor brother is, and how he'll drink and drink for weeks together. Well, Mr. Chantrey's turned in here of an evening, and if Richard was away at the Upton Arms, he's gone after him into the very bar-room itself, and brought him home, just guiding him and handling him like a baby, poor fellow! Often and often he's promised to take the pledge with Richard, but he never could get him to say Yes. No, no! I'd go through fire and water before that should be true."

"Nobody could be sorrier than me," persisted Mrs. Brown, somewhat offended at Ann Holland's vehemence; "I've only told you hearsay, but it comes direct from the cook, and Cousin James only pursed up his mouth. I don't say it's true or it's not true, but nobody in Upton could be sorrier than me if my words come correct. It can't be hidden under a bushel very long, Miss Holland; but I hope as much as you do that it isn't true."

Yet there was an undertone of conviction in Mrs. Brown's manner of speaking that grieved Ann Holland sorely. She accompanied her departing guest to the door, and long after she was out of sight stood looking vacantly down the darkened street. There was little light or sound there now, except in the Upton Arms, where the windows glistened brightly, and the merry tinkling of a violin sounded through the open door. Her brother was there, she knew, and would not be home before midnight. He had been less manageable since Mr. Chantrey went away.

She could not bear to think of Mrs. Chantrey falling into the same sin. The delicate, pretty, refined young lady degrading herself to the level of the poor drunken wretch she called her brother! Ann Holland could not and would not believe it; it seemed too monstrous a scandal to deserve a moment's anxiety. Yet when she went back into her lonely kitchen, her eyes were dim with tears, partly for her brother and partly for Sophy Chantrey.

CHAPTER III. WHAT WAS HER DUTY?

Ann Holland was a great favorite with Mrs, Bolton. The elderly, old-fashioned woman held firmly to all old-fashioned ways; knew her duty to God and her duty to her neighbor, as taught by the Church Catechism, and faithfully fulfilled them to the best of her power. She ordered herself lowly and reverently to all her betters, especially to the widow of an archdeacon. No new-fangled, radical notions, such as her drunken brother picked up, could find any encouragement from her. Mrs. Bolton always enjoyed an interview with her, so marked was her deference. She had occasionally condescended to visit Ann Holland in her kitchen, and sit on the projecting angle of the three-cornered chair, a favor duly appreciated by her delighted hostess. Mr. Chantrey ran in often, as he was passing by, partly because he felt a real friendship, for the true-hearted, struggling old maid, and partly to see after her good-for-nothing brother. As Ann Holland had said herself, she was ready to go through fire and water for the sake of these friends and patrons of hers, whose kindness was the brightest element in her life.

After much tearful deliberation, she received upon the daring step of going to Bolton Villa, on an errand to Mrs. Bolton, with a vague hope that she might discover how false this cruel scandal was. There was a bridle of Mrs. Bolton's in the shop, which had been sent for a new curb, and she would take it home herself. Early the next afternoon, therefore. she clad herself in her best Sunday clothes, and made her way slowly along the streets toward the church. It was but slowly for she rarely went out on a week day, when her neighbors' shops were open; and there were too many attractions in the windows for even her anxiety and consciousness of a solemn mission to resist altogether.

The church and the rectory looked so peaceful amid the trees, just tinged with the hues of autumn, that Ann Holland's spirits insensibly revived. There was little sign of life about the rectory, for no one was living in it at present but Mr. Warden, the clergyman who had taken Mr. Chantrey's duty. Ann Holland opened the church-yard gate and strolled pensively up among the graves to the porch, that she might rest a little and ponder over

Brought Home

what she should say to Mrs. Bolton. There was not a grave there that she did not know; those lying under many of the grassy sods were as familiar to her as the men and women now in full life in the neighboring town. Just within sight, near the vestry window was a little mound covered with flowers, where she had seen a little child of David and Sophy Chantrey's laid to rest. A narrow path was worn up to it; more bare and trodden than before Mr. Chantrey had gone away. Ann Holland knew as well as if she had seen her, that the poor solitary mother had worn the grass away.

The church door was open; for Mr. Warden had chosen to make the vestry his study, and had intimated to all the parish that there he might generally be found if any one among them wished to see him in any difficulty or sorrow. Though this was well known, no one of Mr. Chantrey's parishioners had gone to him for counsel; for he was a grave, stern, silent man, whose opinion it was difficult to guess at and impossible to fathom. He was unmarried, and kept no servant, except the housekeeper who had been left in charge of the rectory. All society he avoided, especially that of women. His abruptness and shyness in their presence was painful both to himself and them. To Mrs. Bolton, however, he was studiously civil, and to Sophy, his friend's wife, he would gladly have shown kindness and sympathy, if he had only known how. He often watched her tracing the narrow footworn track to her baby's grave, and he longed to speak some friendly words of comfort to her, but none came to his mind when they encountered each other. No one in Upton, except Ann Holland, had seen, as he had, how thin and wan her face grew; nor had any one noticed as soon as he had done the strangeness of her manner at times, the unsteadiness of her step, and the flush upon her face, as she now and then passed to and fro under the yew-trees. But he had never had the courage to speak to her at such moments; and there was only a mournful suspicion and dread in his heart, which he did his best to hide from himself.

This afternoon Mrs. Bolton had sought him in the vestry, where he had been silently brooding over his parish and its sins and sorrows, in the dim, green light shining through the lattice window, which was thickly overgrown with ivy. Mrs. Bolton was a handsome woman still, always handsomely dressed, as became a wealthy archdeacon's widow. Her presence seemed to fill up the little vestry; and as she occupied his old, high-backed chair, Mr. Warden stood opposite to her, looking down painfully and shyly at the floor on which he stood, rather than at the distinguished personage who was visiting him.

Brought Home

"I come to you," she said, in a decisive, emphatic voice, "as a clergyman, as well as my nephew's confidential friend. What I say to you must go no farther than ourselves. We have no confessional in our church, thank Heaven! but that which is confided to a clergyman, even to a curate, ought to be as sacred as a confession."

"Certainly," answered Mr. Warden, with painful abruptness.

"Sacred as a confession!" repeated Mrs. Bolton. "I must tell you, then, that I am in the greatest trouble about my nephew's wife. You know how ill she was last winter, after he went away. A low, nervous fever, which hung over her for months. She would not listen to my telling David about it, and, indeed, I was reluctant to distress and disturb him about a matter that he could not help. But she is very strange now; very strange and flighty. Possibly you may have observed some change in her?"

"Yes," he replied, still looking down on the floor, but seeing a vision of Sophy pacing the beaten track to the little grave under the vestry window.

"When she was at the worst," pursued Mrs. Bolton, "and I had the best advice in London for her, she was ordered to take the best wine we could get. I told Brown to bring out for her use some very choice port, purchased by the archdeacon years ago. She must have perished without it; but unfortunately—I speak to you as her pastor, in confidence—she has grown fond of it."

"Fond of it?" repeated Mr. Warden.

"Yes," she answered, emphatically; "I leave the cellar entirely in Brown's charge; a very trusty servant; and I find that Mrs. Chantrey has lately been in the habit of getting a great deal too much from him. But she will take anything she can get that will either stupefy or excite her. She never writes to David until her spirits are raised by stimulants of one kind or another. It is a temptation I cannot understand. I take a proper quantity, just as when the archdeacon was alive, and I never think of exceeding that. I need no more, and I desire no more. But Mrs. Chantrey grows quite excited, almost violent at times. It makes me more anxious than words can express."

There was a long pause, Mr. Warden neither lifting his head nor opening his mouth. His pale face flushed a little, and his lips quivered. David Chantrey was his dearest friend,

Brought Home

and an almost intolerable sense of shame and dread kept him silent. His wife, of whom he always spoke so tenderly in all his letters to him! The very spot where he was listening to this charge against her, David's vestry, seemed to deepen the shame of it, and the unutterable sorrow, if it should be true.

"What would you counsel me to do?" asked Mrs. Bolton, after a time. "Must I write to my nephew and tell him?"

"Do!" he cried, with sudden eagerness and emphasis; "do! Take the temptation out of her way at once. Let everything of the kind be removed from the house. Let no one touch it, or mention it in her presence. Guard her as you would guard a child from taking deadly poison."

"Impossible!" exclaimed Mrs. Bolton. "Have no wine in my house? You forget my station and its duties, Mr. Warden, I must give dinner parties occasionally; I must allow beer to my servants. It is absurd. Nobody could expect me to take such a step as that."

"Listen to me," he said, earnestly, and with an authority quite at variance with his ordinary shyness. "I do not venture to hope for any other remedy. I have known men, ay, and women, who have not dared to pass close by the doors of a tavern for fear lest they should catch but the smell of it, and become brutes again in spite of themselves. Others have not dared even to think of it. If Mrs. Chantrey be falling into this sin, there is no other course for you to pursue than to banish it from your table, and, if possible, from your house. It is better for her to die, if needs be, than to live a drunkard."

"A drunkard!" echoed Mrs. Bolton. "I am sure I never used such a word about Sophy. I cannot believe it possible that my nephew's wife, a clergyman's wife, could become a drunkard, like a woman of the lowest classes! And I cannot understand how you, a clergyman, could seriously propose so extraordinary a step. Why, there is no danger to me; nobody could ever suspect me of being fond of wine. I have taken it in moderation all my life, and I cannot believe it is my duty to give it up altogether at my age."

"Very possibly it has never been your duty before," answered Mr. Warden, "and now I urge it, not for your own sake, but for hers. She has fallen into the snare blindfolded, and you can extricate her, though at some cost to yourself. I feel persuaded you can induce her to abstain, if you will do so yourself. You call yourself a Christian—"

Brought Home

"I should think there can be no doubt about that," she interrupted, indignantly; "the archdeacon never expressed any doubt about it, and surely I may depend upon his judgment."

"Forgive me," said Mr. Warden. "I ought to have said you are a Christian, and a Christian is one who follows his Lord's example."

"Who drank wine himself, and blessed it," interposed Mrs. Bolton, in a tone of triumph.

"The great law of whose life was self-sacrifice," he pursued. "If one of his brethren or sisters had been a drunkard, can you think of him filling up his own cup with wine and drinking it, as they sat side by side at the same table?"

"I should be shocked at imagining anything so presumptuous, not to call it blasphemous," she said. "We can only go by the plain words of Scripture, which tell us that He turned water into wine, and that He drank wine Himself. I am not afraid of going by the plain words of Scripture."

"But we have only fragments of His history," replied Mr. Warden, "and only a few verses of His teachings. Would you say that Paul had more of the spirit of self-sacrifice than Christ? Yet he said, 'It is good neither to eat flesh, nor to drink wine, nor anything whereby thy brother stumbleth.' And again, 'If meat make my brother to offend, I will eat no flesh while the world standeth.' If the servant spoke so, what do you think the Master would have answered if any one had asked Him, 'Lord, what shall I do to save my brother from drunkenness?' It will be a self-denial to you; people will wonder at it, and talk about you; yet I say, if you would truly follow your Lord and Saviour, there is no choice for you. You can save a soul for whom Christ died; and is it possible that you can refuse to do it?"

"I thought," said Mrs. Bolton, "that you would expostulate with her, and warn her as her pastor; and I cannot but believe that, now I have made it known to you, you are responsible for her—at least more responsible than I am. You must use your influence with her; and if she is deaf to reason, we have done all we could."

"I cannot accept the responsibility," he answered, in a tone of pain. "If she were dwelling under my roof, it would be mine; but I cannot take your share of it. As your pastor, I place your duty before you, and you cannot neglect it without peril. As a snare to her soul it has become an accursed thing in your household; and I warn you of it most earnestly, beseeching you to hear in time to save yourself, and her, and David from misery!"

"Mr. Warden," exclaimed Mrs. Bolton, "I am astonished at your fanaticism!"

She had risen from her chair, and was about to sail out of the vestry with an air of outraged dignity, when Mr. Warden said, in a low tone, and with a heavy sigh, "See, there she is!"

Mrs. Bolton paused and turned toward the window, which overlooked the little grave of her nephew's child, who had been very dear to herself. Sophy had just sunk down beside it. There was a slight strangeness and disorder about her appearance, which no stranger might have noticed, but which could not fail to strike both of them. She looked dejected and unhappy, and hid her face in her hands, as though she felt their gaze upon her. The clergyman laid his hand upon Mrs. Bolton's arm with an unconscious pressure, and looked earnestly into her clouded face.

"Look!" he said. "In Christ's name, I implore you to save her."

"I will do what I can," she answered impatiently, "but I cannot take your way to do it; it is irrational."

"There is no other way," he said mournfully, "and I warn you of it."

CHAPTER IV. A BABY'S GRAVE

Sophy Chantrey had strayed absently down to the churchyard in one of those fits of restlessness and nervous despondency which made it impossible to her to remain in the overcrowded rooms of Bolton Villa or in the trim flower-garden surrounding it. There was a continual vague sense of misery in her lot, which she had not strength enough to cast off; but at this moment she was not consciously mourning either for her lost little one or for the absence of her husband and boy. The sharpness and bitterness of her trouble were dulled, and her brain was confused. Even this was a relief from the heavy-heartedness that oppressed her at other times, and she felt a comparative comfort in sitting half-asleep by her child's grave, dreaming confusedly of happier days. She started almost fretfully when Ann Holland's voice broke in upon her drowsy languor.

"Begging your pardon, Mrs. Chantrey," she said, "but I thought I might make bold to ask what news you've had from Mr. Chantrey in Madeira?"

"David!" she answered absently; "David! Oh yes, I see. You are Miss Holland, and he was always fond of you. Do you remember him bringing me to see you just after our marriage? He is getting quite well very fast, thank you. It is only eight months now till he comes home; but that is a long time."

The tears had gathered in her blue eyes, and fell one after another down her cheeks as she looked up pitifully into Ann Holland's kindly face.

"Ah! it is a long time, my dear," she replied, sitting down beside her, though she had some dread of the damp grass; "but we must all of us have patience, you know, and hope on, hope ever. Dear, dear! to think how overjoyed he'll be, and how happy all the folks in Upton will be, when he comes back! It was hard to part with him; but when we see him again, strong and hearty, all that'll be forgot."

"Oh, I've missed him so!" cried Sophy, with a burst of tears; "I've been so solitary without him or Charlie. You cannot think what it is. Sometimes I feel as if they were both dead, and I was doomed to live here without them for ever and ever. Everything seems ended. It is a dreadful feeling."

"And then, dear love," said Ann Holland, in her quietest tones, "I know you just fall down on your knees, and tell God all about it. That's how I do when my poor brother behaves so bad, taking every penny, and pawning or selling all he can lay hands on, to spend in drink. But you know better than me, with all your learning, and music, and painting, and pretty manners, let alone being a clergyman's wife; and when you are that lonesome and sorrowful, you kneel down and tell God all about it."

"No, no," sobbed Sophy, hiding her face again in her hands; "I am so miserable—too miserable to be good, as I used to be when David was at home."

Brought Home

The almost pleasant drowsiness was over now, and a swift tide of thought and memory swept through her brain. The gulf on whose verge she stood seemed to open before her, and she looked down into it shudderingly. She could recollect the temptation assailing her once before, when her baby died; but then her husband was beside her, and his presence had saved her, though not even he had guessed at her danger. What could save her now, alone, with a perpetual weariness of spirit, and a feeling of physical weakness amounting to positive pain? Yet if she went but a few steps forward, she would sink into the gloomy depths, which for the moment her quickened conscience could so clearly perceive. If David could but be at home now! If she could but have her little son to occupy her time and thoughts!

"Dear, dear!" said Ann Holland's low and tender voice; "nobody's too miserable for God not to love them. Why, a poor thing like me can love my brother when he's as bad as bad can be with drink. I could do anything for him out of pity; and it's hard to think less of Him that made us. Sure He knows how difficult it is to be good when we are miserable; and we can't tire Him out. He'll help us out of our misery if we keep stretching out our hands to Him. Nobody knows but Him what we've all got to go through. It's because you're lonesome, and fretting after old days. But they'll come back again, dear love and we'll all be as happy as happy can be. I know how you miss Mr. Chantrey, for I miss him badly, and what must it be for you?"

Sophy lifted up her face, wet with tears, yet with a smile breaking through them. Ann Holland's simple words of comfort and hope had gone direct to her heart, and it seemed possible for her to wait patiently now until David came home.

"You've done me good," she said, "and I shall tell David next time I write to him."

"Dear, dear!" said Ann Holland, with a tone of surprise and pleasure in her voice, "couldn't I do something better for you? Couldn't I just go over to Master Charlie's school, and take him a cake and a little whip out of the shop? It would do me good, worlds of good; and he'd be glad, poor little fellow! Mr. Chantrey's so good to my poor brother; he'd save him from drink if he'd be saved, I know. I'd do anything for your sake or Mr. Chantrey's. But there's Mrs. Bolton coming out of the church, and I've a little business with her; so I'll say good–day to you now, Mrs. Chantrey."

Brought Home

If at this point of her life Sophy Chantrey could have been removed from the daily temptations which beset her, most probably she would not have fallen lower into the degrading sin, which was quickly becoming a habit. Until her husband's enforced absence, she had been so carefully hedged in by the numberless small barriers of a girl's sphere, so guided and managed for by those about her, that it had been hardly possible for any sore temptation to come near her. But now suddenly cut adrift from her quiet moorings, she found herself powerless to keep out of the rapid current which must plunge her into deep misery and vice. There had not been a doubt in her mind that she was not a real Christian, for she had freely given a sentimental faith to the Christian dogmas propounded to her by persons whom she held to be wiser and better than herself. In the same manner she had taken the customs and usages of modern life, always feeling satisfied to do what others of her own class and rank did. Even now, though she was conscious that there was some danger for herself, she could not realize the half of the peril in which she stood. After Ann Holland left her she lingered still beside the little grave in a tranquil but somewhat purposeless reverie. There could be no harm, she thought, in taking just enough to deliver her from her very worst moments of depression, or when she had to write cheerfully to her husband. That was a duty, and she must keep a stricter guard over herself than she had done lately. She would take exactly what her aunt Bolton drank, and then she could not go wrong. With this resolution she gathered a flower from the little grave beside her, and, turning away, hastened out of the churchyard.

Mr. Warden had scarcely glanced through the vestry window since Mrs. Bolton had gone away in anger, but he was well aware of Sophy's lingering beside the grave. He felt crushed and unhappy. His friend Chantrey had solemnly committed the parish to his care, and he to the utmost of his power had strenuously fulfilled his duties. But what was he to do with this new case? Except under strong excitement his constitutional shyness kept him dumb, and how was he to venture to expostulate with his friend's wife upon such a subject? It seemed to be his duty to do something to prevent this lonely and sorrowful girl from drifting into a commonplace and degrading phase of sin. But how was he to begin? How could he even hint at such a suspicion? Besides, he could do nothing to remove her out of temptation. So long as Mrs. Bolton persisted in her angry refusal to follow his advice, she must be exposed daily to indulge an appetite which she had not the firmness to resist.

CHAPTER V. TOWN'S TALK

Perhaps no two persons, outside that nearest circle of kinship which surrounds us all, ever suffered more grief and anxiety in witnessing the slow but sure downfall of a fellow-being, than did Mr. Warden and Ann Holland while watching the gradual working of the curse that was destroying David Chantrey's wife.

It was a miserable time for Mr. Warden. Now and then he accepted Mrs. Bolton's formal invitations to dine with her, and those few acquaintances who were considered worthy to visit at Bolton Villa. On the first occasion he had gone with a faint hope that she had thought over his advice, and resolved to act upon it. But there had been no such result of his solemn warning, which had been so painful to him to deliver. He abstained from taking wine himself, as he believed Christ would have done for the sake of any one so tempted to sin; but his example had no weight. There was a pleasant jest or two at his asceticism, and that was all. Sophy Chantrey took wine as the others did; and, in spite of her resolution, more than the others did; whilst Mrs. Bolton raised her eyebrows, and drew down the corners of her lips, with an air of rebuke. No one knew the meaning of that look except Mr. Warden. The other guests were only entertained by Mrs. Chantrey's fine flow of merry humor, and remarked how well she bore her husband's absence.

"You saw her, Mr. Warden?" said Mrs. Bolton to him, in a low voice, when they reassembled in the drawing-room.

"Yes," he answered, sorrowfully.

"You saw how I looked at her as much as to warn her," pursued Mrs. Bolton. "I am sure she understood me, yet she allowed Brown to fill her glass again and again. What could I do more? I have spoken to her in private; I could not speak to her before our friends."

"I have told you before," he answered, "there is only one thing you can do, and you refuse to do it."

"It would be ridiculous to do it," she said, sharply. "I am not going to make myself a laughing-stock to all the world; and I cannot shut her up in her room, and send her meals to her like a naughty child. You ought to remonstrate with her."

Brought Home

"I will," he replied, "but it will be of little use, so long as the temptation is there. Have you seriously and prayerfully thought of your own duty as a Christian, in this case? Are you quite sure you are acting as Christ himself would have done?"

"None of us can act as He would have, done," she answered, moving from away him. Yet her conscience was uneasy. There was, of a truth, no doubt in her mind as to what the Lord would have done. Yet she could not break through the habits of a lifetime; no, not even to save the wife of her favorite nephew. She did not like to give up the hospitable custom. Her wines were good, bought from the archdeacon's own wine–merchant, and she enjoyed them herself, and liked to hear her guests praise them. No question as to the lawfulness of such an enjoyment had ever arisen before now; but now it troubled her secretly, though she was resolved not to give way. If Sophy Chantrey could not keep within proper limits, it was no fault of hers, and no one could blame her for preserving a harmless custom.

It was not long before Mr. Warden found an opportunity of speaking to Sophy, though it was an agony to him to do it. A few words only were spoken before she knew what he meant to say, and she interrupted him passionately.

"Oh! if David was but here!" she cried, "I could keep right then. But I cannot bear it; indeed, I cannot bear it. The house is so dreary, and there is nothing for me to think of; and then I begin to go down, down into such a misery you do not know anything of. I think I should go mad without it; and after I have taken it, I feel mad with shame. Aunt Bolton has told me what she said to you; and I can hardly bear to look either of you in the face. What shall I do?"

"You must break yourself of the habit," he said pitifully; "God will help you, if you only keep Him in your thoughts. Promise me you will neither taste it, nor look at it again, and I will take the same solemn pledge with you now, before God."

"It would be of no use," she answered, in a hopeless tone, "the instant I see it, I long for it; and I cannot resist the longing. I've vowed on my knees not to take any for a day only; and the moment I have sat down to dinner, I could hardly bear to wait till Brown comes around. If I wake in the night—and I wake so often!—I think of it the first thing. If I could get right away from it, perhaps there might be a chance; but how can I get away?"

Brought Home

"Have you ever thought of what it must lead to?" he asked, wondering at the power the terrible sin had already gained over her.

"Thought!" she cried, "I think of it constantly. David will hate me when he comes home, if I cannot conquer it before then. But what am I to do? I cannot write to him unless I take it. No; I cannot even pray to God, when I am so utterly miserable. It would be better for me to be some poor man's wife, and drudge for my husband and children, than to have nothing to do, and be so much alone. There must be some way of escaping from it; but I cannot find it."

This way of escape—how could he find it for her? It was a question that occupied his thoughts day and night. There was one way, but Mrs. Bolton firmly persisted in closing it, and no other seemed open to her. He could not make known this difficulty to his friend, David Chantrey; for it would be a death-blow to him literally. He would hasten home from Madeira, at the very worst season of the year, as it was now late in October, The risk for him would be too great. There was no other home open to Sophy; and it did not seem possible to make any change in the conditions of that home. She must still be lonely and miserable, and still be exposed to daily temptations. All he could do was so little, that he did it without hope in the results.

If possible, Ann Holland was yet more troubled than he was. By and by it became common town's-talk, and many a neighbor visited her with the purpose of gossiping about poor Mrs, Chantrey. But they found her averse to dwell upon the subject, as if gossip had suddenly grown distasteful to her. Many an hour when she was waiting for her drunken brother to come in from the Upton Arms, she pondered over what she could do to save the wife of her beloved Mr. Chantrey. She knew better than Mr. Warden, who had never been in close domestic contact with the sin, how terrible and repulsive was the degradation of it; and she was heart-sick for Sophy and her husband.

"There's one thing I've done," she said one day to Mrs. Bolton, speaking to her of her brother's drunkenness; "he's never seen me drink a drop of it since he came home drunk the first time. I hate the very sight of it, or to hear people talk of the good it's done them! Why, if it did me worlds of good, and made my poor Richard the miserable wretch he is, I couldn't touch it. And he knows it; he knows I do it for his sake, and maybe he'll turn some day. But if he doesn't turn, I couldn't touch what is ruining him."

Brought Home

"That's very well in your station, Ann," answered Mrs. Bolton, "but it is quite different with us. We owe a duty to society, which must be discharged."

"Very likely, ma'am," she replied meekly; "it's my feelings I was speaking of, not exactly my duty. I hate the name of it; and to think of the thousands and thousands of folks it ruins! When you've seen anybody belonging to you ruined by it you'll hate it, I know. But pray God that may never be!"

"Ann," said Mrs. Bolton, cautiously, "do you suppose any one belonging to me could ever drink more than is right?"

"It's the town's–talk," answered Ann Holland, bursting into tears; "everybody knows it. Oh! Mrs. Bolton, if you can do anything to help her, now is the time to do it. It will get too hard to be rooted up by and by. I know that by my poor brother. He'll never leave it off till he's on his deathbed and can't get it. James Brown, your butler, ma'am, is always talking to him, and exciting him about what he's got charge of in your cellars; and they sit here talking about it for an hour at a time, till they go off to the Upton Arms. I hate the very sound of it."

"But I must have cellars, and I must have a butler," said Mrs. Bolton, somewhat angrily. She was fond of Ann Holland, and liked the reverence she had always paid to her. But this ridiculous notion of Mr. Warden's seemed to have taken possession of the poor, uneducated woman's brain, and threatened to undermine her influence over her. She cut short her visit to her at this point, and returned home uncomfortable and disturbed, wishing she had never offered the shelter of her roof to her nephew's unhappy and weak–minded wife.

Presently, as the dreary winter wore away, Mr. Warden began to shun the sight of Sophy Chantrey. All his efforts to save her, or even to check her rapid downfall, had proved vain; and he turned from her sin with a resentment tinged with disgust. But Ann Holland could feel no resentment or disgust. If it had been in her power she would have watched over her and cared for her night and day with unwearied tenderness. As far as she could she sought to keep alive within her all kinds of softening and pleasant influences. She went often to see Charlie at school, sometimes persuading Sophy to go with her, though more often the unhappy mother shrank from meeting her little son's innocent greetings and caresses. The terrible fits of depression which followed every indulgence of her craving frequently unfitted her for any exertion. She clung to Ann Holland's faithful friendship; but it was not near enough or strong enough to keep her from yielding when she was tempted.

But Sophy Chantrey had not yet fallen to the lowest depths—perhaps never would fall. Her husband's return would save her. Ann Holland looked forward to it as the only hope.

CHAPTER VI. THE RECTOR'S RETURN

David Chantrey's term of exile was over, and the spring had brought release to him. He was returning to England in stronger health and vigor than he had enjoyed for some years before his absence. It seemed to himself that he had completely regained the strength that had been his as a young man. He was a young man yet, he told himself—not six and thirty, with long years of happy work lying before him. The last eighteen months had been weary ones, though he could not count them as lost time, since they had restored him to health. The voyage home was a succession of almost perfectly happy days, as he dwelt beforehand upon the joy that awaited him. He had a packet of letters, those which had reached him from home during his absence; and he read them through once more in the long leisure hours of the voyage. Those from his friend Warden and his aunt which bore a recent date had certainly a rather unsatisfactory tone; but all of Sophy's had been brighter and more cheerful than he had anticipated. Every one of them longed for his return, that was evident. Even Warden, who did not know where his fate would take him to next, expressed an almost extravagant anxiety for his speedy presence in his own parish.

He loved his parish and his people with a peculiar pride and affection. It was twelve years since he had gone to Upton—a young man just in orders, and in the full glow of a fresh enthusiasm as to his duties. He believed no office to be equal to that of a minister of Christ. And though this glow had somewhat passed away, the enthusiasm had deepened rather than faded with the lapse of years, His long illness and exclusion from his office had imparted to it a graver tone. In former days, perhaps, he had been too much set upon the outer ceremonials of religion. He had been proud of his church and the overflowing congregation which assembled in it week after week testifying to his popularity. To pass along the streets of his little town, and receive everywhere the tokens of respect that greeted him, had been exceedingly pleasant. He had bent himself to win golden opinions, after quoting the words of Paul, "I am made all things to all men, that by all means I might save some." And he had succeeded in gaining the esteem of almost every class of his parishioners.

But during the long and lonely months of absence he had learned to love his people after a different fashion. There were some pleasant vices in his parish to which he had shut his eyes; some respectable delinquents with whom he had been on friendly terms, without using his privilege as a friend to point out their misdeeds. There was not a high tone of morality in his parish. Possibly he had been too anxious to please his people. He was going back to them with a deeper and stronger glow of enthusiasm concerning his duties and work among them; but with a graver sense of his own weakness, and a more humble knowledge of the Divine Father for whom he was an ambassador.

His vessel reached Southampton the day before its arrival could have been expected, and neither Sophy nor his friend Warden was there to welcome him. But this was an additional pleasure; he would take them all by surprise in the midst of their preparations for his return. Warden had warned him that there would be quite a public reception of him, with a great concourse of his parishioners, and every demonstration of rejoicing. It was in his nature to enjoy this; but still he would like a few quiet hours with Sophy first, and these he could secure by hastening home by the first train. He would reach Upton early in the evening.

It was an hour of intense happiness, and he felt it to his inmost soul. All the route was familiar to him after he had started from London; the streets and suburbs rushing past him swiftly, and the meadows, in the bright green and gold of spring, which followed them. He knew the populous villages, with their churches, where he was himself well known. Every station seemed almost like a home to him. As he drew nearer to Upton he leaned through, the window to catch the first glimpse of his own church, and the blue smoke rising from his own house; and a minute or two afterward, with a gladness that was half a pain, he found himself once more on the platform at Upton station.

"I am back again," he said, shaking hands with the station-master with a hearty grasp that spoke something of his gladness. "Is all going on well among you?"

"Yes, Mr. Chantrey; yes, sir," he answered. "You're welcome home, sir. God bless you! You've been missed more than any of us thought of when you went away. You're needed

Brought Home

here, sir, more than you think of."

"Nothing has gone very wrong, I hope," said the rector, smiling. He had faithfully done his best to provide a good substitute in "Warden, but it was not in human nature not to feel pleased that no one could manage his parish as well as himself.

"No, no, sir," replied the station-master, "nothing but what you'll put right again at once by being at home yourself. No, there's nothing very wrong, I may say. Upton meant to give you a welcome home to-morrow, with arches of flowers and music. They'll be disappointed you arrived to-day, I know."

David Chantrey laughed, thinking of the welcome they had given him when he brought Sophy home as his young wife. His heart felt a new tenderness for her, and a throb of impatience to find her. He bade a hasty good-evening to the station-master, and walked off buoyantly toward the High street, along which his path lay. The station-master and the ticket-clerk watched him, and shook their heads significantly; but he was quite unconscious of their scrutiny. Never had the quiet little town seemed so lovely to him. The quaint irregular houses stood one-half of them in shadow, and the rest in the level rays of the May sunset; the chestnut-trees, with their young green leaves and their white blossoms lighting up each branch to the very summit of them; the hawthorn bushes here and there covered with snowy bloom; the children playing, and the swallows darting to and fro overhead; the distant shout of the cuckoo, and the deep low tone of the church clock just striking the hour—this was the threshold of home to him; the outer court, which was dearer to him and more completely his own than any other place in the wide world could ever be.

No one was quick to recognize him in his somewhat foreign aspect; the children at their play took no notice of him. All the tradespeople were busy getting their shops a little in order before the shutters were put up. He might perhaps pass through the street as far as Bolton Villa without being observed, and so be sure of a perfectly quiet evening. But as he thought so his heart gave a great bound, for there before him was Sophy herself hurrying along the uneven causeway, now lost behind some jutting building, and then seen once more, still hastening with quick, unsteady steps, as if bent on some pressing errand. He did not try to overtake her, though he could have done so easily. He felt that their first meeting must not be in the street, for the tears that smarted under his eyelids and dimmed his sight, and the quicker throbbing of his pulses, warned him that such a meeting would be no common incident in their lives. She had been his wife for nine years, and she was far dearer to him now than she had been when he married her. Eighteen months of their life together had been lost—a great price to pay for his restored health. But now a long, happy union lay before them.

He had not followed her for more than a minute or two when she suddenly turned and entered Ann Holland's little shop. Well, he could not take her by surprise better in any other house in Upton. Perhaps it might even be better than at Bolton Villa, amid its cumbrous surroundings; he always thought of his aunt's house with a sort of shudder. If Sophy had fortunately fixed upon this quiet house for paying the good old maid a kindly visit, there was not another place except their own home where he would rather receive her first greeting—that is if the drunken old saddler did not happen to be in. He paused to inquire from the journeyman, still at work in the shop; learning that Richard Holland was not at home, he passed impatiently to the kitchen beyond. Ann Holland was just closing the door of her little parlor, and David Chantrey approached her, hardly able to control the agitation he felt.

"I saw my wife step in here," he said, holding out his hand to her, but attempting to pass her and to open the door before which she still stood. She could not speak for a moment, but she kept her post firmly in opposition to him.

"My wife is here?" he asked, in a sharp impetuous tone.

"Yes; oh yes!" cried Ann Holland; "but wait a moment, Mr. Chantrey. Oh, wait a little while. Don't go in and see her yet."

"Why not?" he asked again, a sudden terror taking hold of him.

"Sit down a minute or two, sir," she answered. "Mrs. Chantrey's ill, just ailing a little. She is not prepared to meet you just yet. You were not expected before to-morrow, and she's excited; she hardly knows what she's saying or doing. You'd better not speak to her or see her till she's recovered herself a little."

"Poor Sophy!" cried David Chantrey, with a tremor in his voice; "did she see me coming, then? Go back to her, Miss Holland; she will want you. Is there nothing I can do for her? It has been a hard time for her, poor girl!"

Ann Holland went back into the parlor, and he smiled as he heard her take the precaution of turning the key in the lock. He threw himself into the three-cornered chair, and sat listening to the murmur of voices on the other side of the door. It seemed a very peaceful home. The quaintness and antiqueness of the homely kitchen chimed in with his present feeling; he wanted no display or grandeur. This was no common every-day world he was in; there was a strange flavor about every circumstance. Impatient as he was to see Sophy, and hold her once more in his arms, he could not but feel a sense of comfort and tranquillity mingling with his more unquiet happiness. There was a fire burning cheerily on the hearth, though it was a May evening. Coming from a warmer climate, he felt chilly, and he bent over the fire, stretching over it his long thin hands, which told plainly their story of mere scholarly work and of health never very vigorous, Smiling all the time, with the glow of the flame on his face, with its expression of tranquil gladness, as of one who had long been buffeted about, but had reached home at last, he sat listening till the voices ceased. A profound silence followed, which lasted some time, before Ann Holland returned to him saying softly, "She is asleep."

CHAPTER VII. WORSE THAN DEAD

Ann Holland sat down on the other side of the hearth, opposite her rector; but she could not lift up her eyes to his face. There was no on in the world whom she loved so well. His forbearance and kindness toward her unfortunate brother, who was the plague and shame of her life, had completely won for him an affection that would have astonished him if he could have known its devotion. This moment would have been one of unalloyed delight to her had there been no trouble lurking for him, of which he was altogether unaware. So rejoiced she was at his return that it seemed as if no event in her monotonous life hitherto had been so happy; yet she was terrified at the very thought of his coming wretchedness. When Sophy had fled to her with the cry that her husband was come, and she dared not meet him as she was, she had seen in an instant that she must prevent it by some means or other. The hope that Mr. Chantrey's return would bring about a reformation in his wife had grown faint in her heart, for during the last few months the sin had taken deeper and deeper root; and now, the day only before she expected him, she had not had strength to resist the temptation to it. Sophy had been crying hysterically, and trembling at the thought of meeting him as she was; and she had made Ann promise to break to him gently the confession she would otherwise be compelled to make herself. Ann Holland sat opposite to him, with downcast eyes, and a face almost heart-broken by the shame and sorrow she foresaw for him.

"She is asleep," he said, repeating her words in a lowered voice, as if he was afraid of disturbing her.

"Yes," she answered.

"It is strange," he said, after a short pause; "strange she can sleep now. Has she been ill? Sophy always assured me she was quite well and strong. It is strange she can sleep when she knows I am here."

"She was very ill and low after you went, sir," she replied; "it was like as if her heart was broken, parting with you and Master Charlie both together. Dear, dear! it might have been better for her if you'd been poor folks, and she'd had to work hard for you both. She'd just nothing to do, and nobody to turn to for comfort, poor thing. Mrs. Bolton meant to be kind, and was kind in her way: but she fell into a low fever, and the doctors all ordered her as much wine and support as ever she could take."

"I never heard of it," said Mr. Chantrey; "they never told me."

"No; they were fearful of your coming back too soon," she went, on; "and, thank God, you are looking quite yourself again, sir. All Upton will be as glad as glad can be, and the old church'll be crammed again. Mr. Warden's done all a man could do; but everybody said he wasn't you and we longed for you back again, but not too soon—no, no, not too soon."

"But my wife," he said; "has she been ill all the time?"

For a minute or two she could not find words to answer his question. She knew that it could not be long before he learned the truth, if not from her or his wife, then from Mrs. Bolton or his friend Mr. Warden. It was too much the common talk of the neighborhood for him to escape hearing of it, even if she could hope that Mrs. Chantrey would have strength of mind enough to cast off the sin at once. Now was the time to break it to him gently, with quiet and friendly hints rather than with hard words. But how was she to do it? How could she best soften the sorrow and disgrace?

Brought Home

"Is my wife ill yet?" he demanded again, in a more agitated voice.

"Not ill now," she answered, "but she's not quite herself yet. You'll help her, sir. You'll know how to treat her kindly and softly, and bring her round again. There's a deal in being mild and patient with folks. You know my poor brother, as fierce as a tiger, and that obstinate, tortures would not move him; but he's like a lamb with you, Mr. Chantrey. I think sometimes if he could live in the same house with you, if he'd been your brother, poor fellow you'd save him; for he'll do anything for you, short of keeping away from drink. You'll bring Mrs. Chantrey round, I'm sure."

Mr. Chantrey smiled again, as the comparison between the drunken old saddler and his own fair, sweet young wife, flitted across his brain. Ann Holland, in her voluble flow of words, hit upon curious combinations. Still she had not removed his anxiety about his wife. "Was Sophy suffering from the effects of the low, nervous fever yet?

"Yes; I'll take care of my wife," he said, glancing toward the parlor door; "it has been a sore trial, this long separation of ours. But it's over now; and she is dearer to me than ever she was."

"Ay! love will do almost everything," she answered, sadly, "and I know you will never get tired or worn out, if it's for years and years. A thing like this doesn't come right all at once; but if it comes right at last, we have cause to be thankful. Mr. Warden has not had full patience; and Mrs. Bolton lost hers too soon. Neither of them knows it as I know it. You can't storm it away; and it's no use raving at it. Only love and patience can do it; and not that always. But we are bound to bear with them, poor things! even to death. We cannot measure God's patience with our measure."

Ann Holland's voice trembled, and her eyes filled with tears, which glistened in the firelight. She could not bear to speak more plainly to her rector, whom she loved and reverenced so greatly. She could not think of him as being brought down on a level with herself, the sister of a known drunkard. It seemed a horrible thing to her; this sorrow hanging over him, of which he was so utterly unconscious. Mr. Chantrey had fastened his eyes upon her as if he would read her inmost thoughts. His voice trembled a little too, when he spoke.

Brought Home

"What has this to do with my wife?" he asked, "for what reason have my aunt and Mr. Warden lost patience with her?"

"Oh! it's best for me to tell you, not them," she said, the tears streaming down her cheeks; "it will be very hard for you to hear, whoever says it. Everybody knows it; and it could never be kept from you. But you can save her, Mr. Chantrey, if anybody can. It's best for me to tell you at once. She was so ill, and low, and miserable; and the doctors kept on ordering her wine, and things like that; and it was the only thing that comforted her, and kept her up; and she got to depend upon it to save her from loneliness and wretchedness, and now she can't break herself of taking it—of taking too much."

"Oh! my God!" cried Mr. Chantrey. It was a cry from the very depths of his spirit, as by a sudden flash he saw the full meaning of Ann Holland's faltered words. Sophy had fled from him, conscious that she was in no fit state to meet him after their long separation. She was sleeping now the heavy sleep of excess. Was it possible that this was true? Could it be anything but a feverish dream that he was sitting there, and Ann Holland was telling him such an utterly incredible story? Sophy, his wife, the mother of his child!

But Ann Holland's tearful face, with its expression of profound grief and pity, was too real for her story to be a dream. He, David Chantrey, the rector of Upton, whom all men looked up to and esteemed, had a wife, who was whispered about among them all as a victim to a vile and degrading sin. A strong shock of revulsion ran through his veins, which had been thrilling with an unquiet happiness all the day. There was an inexplicable, mysterious misery in it. If he had come home to find her dead, he could have borne to look upon her lying in her coffin, knowing that life could never be bright again for him; but he would have held up his head among his fellow-men. It would have been no shame or degradation either for him or her to have laid her in the tranquil churchyard, beside their little child, where he could have seen her grave through his vestry window, and gone from it to his pulpit, facing his congregation, sorrowful but not disgraced. He was just coming back to his people with higher aims, and greater resolves, determined to fight more strenuously against every form of evil among them; and this was the first gigantic sin, which met him on his own threshold and his own hearth.

"She's so young," pleaded Ann Holland, frightened at the ashy hue that had spread over his face, "and she's been so lonesome. Then it was always easy to get it, when she felt low; for Mrs. Bolton's servants rule the house, and there's the best of everything in her cellars. James Brown says he could never refuse Mrs. Chantrey, she was so miserable, poor thing! But now you will take her home; and she'll have you, and Master Charlie. You'll save her, sir, sooner or later; never fear."

"Let me go and see her," he said, in a choking voice.

Ann Holland opened the door so carefully that the latch did not click or the hinges creak; and, shading the light with her hand, she stood beside him for a minute or two, as he looked down upon his sleeping wife. She did not dare to lift her eyes to his face; but she knew that all the light and glow of gladness had fled from it, and a gray look of terror had crept across it. He was a very different man from the one who had been seated on her hearth a short half-hour ago. He bade her leave him alone, and without a light, and she obeyed him, though reluctantly, and with an undefined fear of him in his wretchedness.

It seemed to Mr. Chantrey as if an age had passed over him. As persons who are drowning see in one brief moment all the course of their past lives, with its most trivial circumstances, so he seemed to have looked into his own future, stretching before him in gloom and darkness, and foreseen a thousand miserable results springing from this fatal source. She was his wife, dearer to him than any other object in the world; but after she had repented and reformed, as surely she would repent and reform, she could never be to him again what she had been. There Was a faint gleam of moonlight stealing into the familiar room, and he could just distinguish her form lying on the white-covered sofa. With an overwhelming sense of wretchedness and bewilderment he fell upon his knees beside her, and burying his face in his hands, cried again, "Oh! my God!"

CHAPTER VIII. HUSBAND AND WIFE

How long he knelt there, Mr. Chantrey did not know. He felt cramped and stiff, for he did not stir from his first position; and he had uttered no other word of prayer. But at last Sophy moved and turned her head; and he lifted up his face at the sound. The moon was shining full into the room, and they could see one another, but not distinctly, as in daylight. She looked at him in dreamy silence for a few moments, and then she timidly stretched out her hand, and whispered, "David!"

"My wife!" he answered, laying his own cold hand upon hers.

Brought Home

For some few minutes neither of them spoke again. They gazed at one another as though some great gulf had opened between them, and neither of them could cross it. In the dim light they could only see the pallid, outline of each other's face, as though they had met in some strange, sad world. But presently he leaned over her, and kissed her.

"Oh!" she cried, with a sudden loudness that rang through the quiet room, "you know all! You know how wicked I am. But you don't know how lonely and wretched I have been. I tried to break myself of it I did try to keep from it; but it was always there on the table when I sat down to my meals with Aunt Bolton; and I could always find comfort in it. Oh! help me! Don't cast me off; don't hate me. Help me."

"I will help you," he answered, earnestly; but he could say no more. The mere sound of the words she spoke unnerved him.

"And I have made you miserable just as you are coming home!" she went on. "I never meant to do that. But I was so restless, looking forward to to–morrow; and aunt's maid advised me to take a little, for fear I should be quite ill when you came. I should have been all right to–morrow; and I was so resolved never to touch it again, after you had come home. You are come back quite strong, are you? There is no more fear for you? Oh! I will conquer myself; I must conquer myself. If it had not always been in my sight, and the doctors had not ordered it, I should never have been so wicked. Do you forgive me? Do you think God will forgive me?"

"Can you give it up?" he asked.

"Oh! I must, I will give it up," she sobbed; "but if I do, and if you forgive me, it can never be the same again. You will not think the same of me—and people have seen me—they all talk about it—and I shall always be ashamed before them. I am a disgrace to you; Aunt Bolton has said so again and again. Then there's Charlie; I'm not fit to be his mother. That is quite true. However long I live, people in Upton will remember it, and gossip about, it. If they had let me die it would have been better for us all. You could have loved me then."

"But I love you still," he answered, in a voice of tenderness and pity; "you are very dear to me. How can I ever cease to love you?"

Brought Home

Yet as he spoke a terrible thought flashed through his mind that his wife might some day become to him an object of unutterable disgust. An image of a besotted, drunken woman always in his house, and bearing his name, stood out for a moment sharply and distinctly before his imagination. He shuddered, and paused; but almost before she could notice it, he went on in low and solemn tones.

"Your sin does not separate you from me; you are my wife. I must help you and save you at whatever cost. Your soul is nearer to mine than any other; and what one human being can do for the soul of another, it is my lot to do. Do not be afraid of me, Sophy. You cannot estrange yourself from me; and yon cannot wear out the patience of God. He is ever waiting to receive back those who have wandered farthest from him. Can I refuse love and pity, when He freely gives them in full measure to you? Will Christ forsake you—He who saved Mary Magdalen? He will cast out this demon that has possession of you."

He was replying to some of the questions which had troubled him, while he was kneeling at her side, before she was awake. There was no separation possible of their lives. If she broke away from him, or if he sent her away from his home, they would still be bound together by ties that could never be broken. Whatever depth she sank to, she was his wife, and he must tread step by step with her the path that ran through all the future. But if any one could help her, and lead her back out of her present bondage, it was he; and he must not fail her in any extremity for lack of pity and tenderness.

He was about to speak again, when a loud, rough noise broke in upon the quiet of the house. It was nearly midnight; and Ann Holland's drunken brother was stumbling and staggering through his shop into the peaceful little kitchen, Sophy sat up and listened. They could hear his thick, coarse voice shouting out snatches of vulgar songs, mingled with oaths at his sister, who was doing her utmost to persuade him to go quietly to bed. His shambling step, dragging across the floor, seemed about to enter the darkened room where they were sitting; and Sophy caught her husband's arm, clinging to it with fright. It was a more bitter moment for Mr. Chantrey than even for her. The comparison thrust upon him was too terrible. His delicate, tender, beloved wife, and this coarse, brutal, degraded man! Was it possible that both were bound by the chains of the same sin?

But Ann Holland succeeded before long in getting her brother out of the way, and releasing them from their painful imprisonment. The streets of Upton were hushed in utter solitude and silence as they walked through them, speechless and heavy-hearted; those streets which, on the morrow, were to have been crowded with groups of his people, eager to welcome him home. They passed the church, lit up with the moonlight, clear enough to make every grave visible; a lovely light, in which all the dead seemed to be sleeping restfully. He sighed heavily as he passed by. Sophy was clinging to him, sobbing now and then; for her agitation had subsided into a weak dejection, which found no relief but in tears. Every step they trod along the too familiar road brought a fresh pang to him. For thousands of memories of happy days haunted him; and a thousand vague fears dogged him. He dared not open his heart either to the memories or the fears. Nothing was possible to him, except a silent, continuous cry to God for help.

"It is a melancholy coming home," Sophy murmured, as they stood together on the threshold of their aunt's house. He had not time to answer, for the door was opened quickly, and Mrs. Bolton hurried forward to welcome him. She had been expecting him for some time, for Ann Holland had sent word that both he and Mrs. Chantrey were at her house. One glance at his anxious and sorrowful face revealed to her the anguish of the last few hours. Sophy crept away guiltily up stairs; and she put her arm through his, and led him into the dining-room, where a luxurious supper was spread for him.

"You know all about it, then?" said Mrs. Bolton, as he threw himself into a chair by the fireside, looking utterly bowed down and wretched.

"Yes," he answered. "Oh! aunt, could you do nothing for her? Could you not prevent it? It is a miserable thing for a man to come back to."

"I have done all I could," she replied, hesitatingly. "I have been quite wretched about it myself; but what could I do? I told your friend Mr. Warden there was nothing in reason I would refuse to do; but his ideas were so impracticable they could not be carried out."

"What were they?" he asked.

"Positively that I should abstain altogether myself," she said; "and not only that, but I must refuse it to my guests, and have nothing of the kind in my house; not even those choice wines your uncle bought, Neither wine for myself nor ale for my servants! It was quite out of the question, you know. Mr. Warden was meddlesome to the very verge of impertinence about it, until I was compelled to give up inviting him to my house. He went so far as to doubt my being a Christian! And it was of no use telling him I followed our Lord's example more strictly by drinking wine than he did by abstaining from it. He used his influence with Sophy to persuade her to suggest the same thing, that I would keep it altogether out of her sight at all times; but she soon saw how impossible it was for a person of my station and responsibility to do such a thing. I told her it was putting total abstinence above religion."

"Did Sophy think that would save her?" asked Mr. Chantrey.

"She had a fancy it would," answered Mrs. Bolton, "but only because Mr. Warden put it into her head. She was quite reasonable about it, poor girl! I proved to her that our Lord did not do it, nor some of the best Christians that ever lived; and she was quite convinced. Even Ann Holland was troublesome about it, begging me to do all kinds of extraordinary things—to have Charlie here was one of them, as if that could cure her—but I soon made her understand her position and mine. I am sure nobody can be more anxious than I am to do what is right. I am afraid it is the development of an hereditary taste in your wife, David, and nothing will cure it; for I have made many inquiries about her family, and I hear several of her relations were given to excess; so you may depend upon it, it is hereditary and incurable."

There was little comfort for him in this speech, which was delivered in a satisfied and judicial tone. Sophy's sin had been present to Mrs. Bolton for so many months, and she had grown so accustomed to analyze it, and argue about it, that she could not enter into the sudden and direful shock the discovery had been to her nephew. An antagonism had risen in her mind about it, not only against Mr. Warden, but against some faint, suppressed reproaches of conscience, which made her secretly cleave to the idea that this vice was hereditary, and consequently incurable. She was afraid also of David reproaching her. But he did not. He was too crushed to reason yet about his wife's fall, or what measures might have been taken to prevent it. Long after his aunt had left him, and not a sound was to be heard in the house, he sat alone, scarcely thinking, but with one deep, poignant, bitter sense of anguish weighing upon his soul. Now and then he cried to God inarticulately; that dumb, incoherent cry of the stricken spirit to the only Saviour.

CHAPTER IX. SAD DAYS

There was no doubt in Upton, when the people saw their rector again, that he knew full well the calamity that had befallen him. No one ventured to speak to him of it; but their very silence was a measure of the gravity of his trouble. His friend Warden told him more accurately than any one else could have done, how it had gradually come about, and what remonstrances he had made both to Mrs. Bolton and Sophy. Mr. Chantrey was impatient to get into his own house, where he could do what his aunt had refused to do, and where he could shield his wife from all temptation to yield to the craving for stimulants in any form. When they were at home once more, with their little son with them, filling up her time and thoughts, all would be well again.

But he did not know the force of the habit she had fallen into. At first there were a few gleams of hope and thankfulness during the pleasant days of summer, while it was a new thing for Sophy to have her husband and child with her. But he could not keep her altogether from temptation, while they visited constantly at Bolton Villa, and the houses of other friends. It was in vain that he abstained himself; that he made himself a fanatic on the question, as all his acquaintances said; Sophy could not go out without being exposed to temptation, and she was not strong enough to resist it. Before the next spring came, the people of Upton spoke of her as confirmed in her miserable failing. There was no one but herself who could now break off this fatal habit; and her will had grown wretchedly feeble. The sin domineered over her, and she felt herself a helpless slave to it. There had been no want of firmness or tenderness on the part of her husband; but it had taken too strong a hold upon her before he came to her aid. The intolerable sense of humiliation which she suffered only drove her to seek to forget it by sinking lower into the depth of her degradation and his.

A great change came over the rector of Upton. He went about among his parishioners, no longer gladly taking the leadership among them, and claiming the pre-eminence as his by right. It had been one of his most pleasant thoughts in former days that he was the rector of the parish, chosen of God, and appointed by men, to teach them truths good for himself and them, and to go before them, seeking out the path in which they should walk. But his own feet were now stumbling upon dark mountains. He was quickly losing his popularity among them; for whereas, while he was himself happy and honored, he had not seen clearly all the evils, and wrongs, and excesses of his parish, now he was growing, as they said, more fanatical and ascetic than Mr. Warden had been, who had won the name of a puritan among them. Why could he not leave the Upton Arms and the numerous smaller taverns alone, so long as the landladies and their daughters attended church, as they had been need to do? His presence at the dinner-parties of his friends was a check upon all hilarity; and by and by they ceased to invite him, and then, half ashamed to see his face, ceased to go to his church, where his sermons had not the smooth and flowery eloquence of former days.

Probably Mr. Chantrey knew better now what was good for his people; he had clearer views of the snares and dangers that beset them, and the sorrows that lie lurking on every man's path. He saw more distinctly what Christ came to do; and how he did it by complete self-abnegation, and by descending to the level of the lowest. But he had no delight in standing up in his pulpit in full face of his dwindling congregation. Language seemed poor to him; and it had grown difficult to him to put his burning thoughts into words. As the bitter experience of daily life seared his very soul, he found that no smooth, fit expressions of his self-communing rose to his lips. It pained him to face his people, and speak to them in old, trite forms of speech, while his heart was burning within him; and they knew it, as they sat quiet in their pews, looking up to him with inquisitive or indifferent eyes.

Mrs, Bolton could not escape her share of these troubles; though she never accused herself for a moment as having had any part in causing them. It was the archdeacon who had obtained the living of Upton for her favorite nephew; and she had settled there to be the patroness of every good thing in the parish. Mr. Chantrey's popularity had been a source of great satisfaction and self-applause to her. She had foreseen how useful he would be; what a shining light in this somewhat dark corner of the church. The increasing congregations, and the number of carriages at the church-door, had given her much pleasure. She had delighted in taking the lead, side by side with her nephew, and in being looked up to in Upton, as one who set an example in every good thing. But this unfortunate failing in her nephew's wife, developed under her roof and during his absence, had been a severe blow. No one directly blamed her for it, except the late curate, Mr. Warden, and a few extravagant, visionary persons, who deemed it best to abstain totally from the source of so much misery and poverty among their fellow-beings, and to take care, as far as in them lay, to place no stumbling-block in the way of feeble feet. But, strange to say, all the estimable people in Upton regarded her with less veneration since her niece had gone astray. Even Ann Holland was plainly less impressed and swayed by the idea of her goodness; and there were many others like Ann Holland. As for her nephew, he was gradually falling away from her in his trouble. He would seldom go to dine with her without Sophy; and he had urgent reasons to decline every invitation for her. Their conversations upon religious subjects, which had always tended to make her comfortably assured of her own state of grace, had quite ceased. David never talked to her now about his sermons, past or future. He was in the "wasteful wilderness" himself, and could not walk with her through trim alleys of the vineyards. Now and then there fell from him, as from his friend, unpractical notions of a Christian's duty; as if Christianity consisted more in acts of self-denial than in an accurate creed concerning fundamental doctrines. It was an uneasy time for Mrs. Bolton; and her chief consolation was found in a volume of sermons, published by the archdeacon, which made her feel sure that all must be right with the widow of such a dignitary.

CHAPTER X. A SIN AND A SHAME

It was May again; a soft, sunny day, with spring showers falling, or gathering in glistening clouds in the blue sky. The bells chimed for morning service, as the people came up to church from the old-fashioned streets. They greeted one another as they met in the churchyard, whispering that it had been a very bad week for poor Mr. Chantrey. Every one knew how uncontrollable his wife had been for some time past, except a few strangers, who still drove in from a distance. The congregation, some curiously, some wistfully, gazed earnestly at him, as with a worn and weary face, and with bowed-down head already streaked with gray, he took his place in the reading-desk. Ann Holland wiped away her tears stealthily, lest he should see she was weeping, and guess the reason. In the rectory pew the young, fair-haired boy sat alone, as he had often done of late; for his mother was to unfit to appear in church.

Mr. Chantrey read the service in a clear, steady voice, but with a tone of trouble in it which only a very dull ear could have missed. When he ascended his pulpit, and looked down with sad and sunken eyes upon his people, every face was lifted up to him attentively, as he gave out the text, "Am I my brother's keeper?" Mrs. Bolton moved uneasily in her pew, for she knew he was going to preach a disagreeable sermon. It was not as eloquent as many of his old ones; but it had a hundredfold more power. His hearers had often been pleased and touched before; now they were stirred, and made uncomfortable. Their responsibilities, as each one the keeper of his brother's soul, were

Brought Home

solemnly laid before them. The listless, contented indifference to the sins and sorrows of their fellow-men was rudely shaken. Their satisfaction in their own safety was attacked. As clearly as words could put it, they were told that not one of them could go to heaven alone; that there was no solitary path of salvation for any foot to tread. As long as any fell because of temptation, they were bound, as far as in them lay, to remove every kind of temptation. If each one was not careful to be his brother's keeper, then the voice of their brother's blood would cry unto God against them. There was scarcely a person present who could listen to their rector's sermon with feelings of self-satisfaction.

He left his pulpit at the close of it, troubled and exhausted. His little son followed him into the vestry to wait until the congregation, that loved to linger a little about the porch, should have dispersed. But hardly had he entered, than, looking out, as it was his wont to do, upon the grave of his other child, he saw a figure stretched across it, asleep. Could it possibly be his wife? Large drops of rain were beginning to fall upon her upturned face, but they did not rouse her from her heavy slumber; nor did the noise of many feet passing by along the churchyard path. It was a moment of unutterable shame and agony to him. His people saw her; they had heard of his trouble before, but now they saw it; and they were lingering to look at her. He must go out in the midst of them all, and they must see him take his miserable wife home.

Those who were there that day will never forget the sight. His people made way for him, as he passed among them, still in the gown he had worn while preaching, with a rigid and wan face, and eyes that seemed blind to every object except the unhappy woman he could not save. His little boy was pressing close behind him, but he bade him go back into the church, and wait until he came for him. Then he knelt down beside his wife in the falling rain, and lifted her gently, calling her by her name, "Sophy! Sophy!" But her heavy head fell back again upon the grave, and he was not strong enough to raise her from it. He burst into tears, a passion of tears; such as men only weep in hours of extreme anguish of mind. Slowly his people melted away, helpless to do anything for him; except two or three of his most familiar friends, who stayed to assist him in taking the wretched wife back to her home.

Ann Holland lingered unseen in the porch until all were out of sight. The child she loved so fondly was standing with the great door ajar, holding it with his small hand, and peeping out now and then. She called to him when all were gone, and he came out of the church gladly, yet with an air of concern on his round, rosy face.

Brought Home

"My mother is ill, very ill," he said, putting his hand into hers. "I saw her lying on baby's grave. Couldn't anything be done for her to make her well? Isn't there any doctor clever enough to cure her?"

"I don't know, dear," answered Ann Holland.

"My father never lets me go to see her when she's worst," he went on, "only Sarah goes into her room, and him. She talks and laughs often, and yet my father says she is ill. When I am a man I shall be a doctor, and learn how to make her well. But it will be a long time before I am clever enough for that, I'm afraid. My father says she's too ill for anybody to come to see us; isn't it a pity?"

"Yes, my dear," she answered.

"She can never hear me say my hymns now," he said; "and when she's not so ill that my father won't let me see her, she sits crying, crying ever so; and if I want to play with her, or read to her, she can't bear it, she says. I should think there ought to be somebody to cure her, if we could only find out. My father scarcely ever laughs now, because she's so ill; and when he plays with me he only looks sad, and he speaks in a quiet voice as if it would make her worse. Do try, Miss Holland, and ask everybody that comes to your house if they don't know of some very, very clever doctor for my mother."

"I will try," she said. "I'll do all I can. But you may run home now, Master Charlie, See! There's your father coming back for you,"

"I know I sha'n't see my mother again to-day," he answered; "good-by, and remember, please."

She watched him running across the little meadow to his father; and then she turned away, and walked slowly through the street homeward. Little knots of the towns-people lingered still about the doorways, discussing their rector's troubles. Though most of them greeted her, anxious to hear her opinion as one who was considered on friendly terms with the rector's family, she evaded their questionings, and passed on to the solitude of her own dwelling. It had been solitary now for some days, for her brother had disappeared early in the week; having stripped the house of money, and set off on one of his vagrant tramps, of which she knew nothing except that he always returned penniless,

Brought Home

and generally with the good clothes she provided for him exchanged for worthless rags. How many years it was that her life had been embittered by his drunkenness she could hardly reckon, so many had they been. These strange absences of his had at first been a severe trial to her; but of late years they had been a holiday time of rest, except for the continual anxiety she felt on his behalf. Her quaint and quiet kitchen, as she unlocked the door and entered it, seemed a haven of refuge, where she could indulge in the tears she had kept under control till now. The love she felt for Mr. Chantrey was so deep and true, that any sorrow of his must have grieved her. But she knew so well what this sorrow was! She knew through what long years it might last; and how hopeless it might grow before the end came. Looking back upon her own blighted life, she could foresee for him only a weary, miserable, ever-deepening wretchedness. The Sunday afternoon passed by slowly, and the evening came, The soft sunshine and spring showers of the morning were gone; and a sullen sweep of rain, driven by the east wind, was beating through the streets. A neighbor looked in to say she had seen the curate from the next parish pass through the town toward the church; and she thought Mr. Chantrey would very likely not be there. But Ann Holland had already decided not to go. At any moment she might hear her brother's shambling step draw near the door, and his fingers fumbling at the latch. She could not bear the neighbors to see him when he came off one of his vagabond tramps, dirty and ragged as he usually was. She must stay at home again for him; again, as she had done hundreds of times, mourning pitifully over him, and ready to receive him patiently, impenitent as he was. She went up stairs to make his bed quite ready for him; and to put out of his way everything that could by any chance hurt him, if he should stumble and fall in his drunken weakness. When she returned to the kitchen, she lighted a candle, and opened the old family Bible, with its large type, which seemed to her a more sacred book than the little one she used daily. But she could not read; the words passed vaguely and without meaning beneath her eyes. Her mind was full of the thought of her unhappy brother, and Mr. Chantrey's miserable wife.

It was past her usual hour of going to bed before she made up the kitchen fire to be in readiness, lest her brother should knock her up at any hour during the night. At the last moment she opened the street-door, and stood listening for a little while, as she always did when he was not at home. The rain was still sweeping through the street, which was as silent as if the town had been deserted. The gas-lights in the lamps flickered with the wind, and lit up the pools and channels of water running down the pavements.

Brought Home

But just as she turned to go in, her quick ear caught the sound of distant footsteps, growing louder as they came in her direction. It was the tramp of several feet, marching slowly like those of persons bearing a heavy burden. She waited to see who and what it could be so late this Sunday night; and soon, under the flickering lamps, she caught sight of several men, carrying among them a hurdle, with a shapeless heap upon it. A sudden, vague panic seized her, and she hastily retreated inside her house, shutting and barring the door. She said to herself she did not wish to see what they were carrying past. But were they going past? She heard them still, tramping slowly on toward her house; would they pass by with their burden? She put down the light, for her hand trembled too much to hold it; and she stood listening, her ears quickened for every sound, and her white face turned toward the closed and fastened door.

A knock came upon it, which almost caused her to shriek aloud. Yet it was a quiet rap, and a neighbor's voice answered as she asked tremulously who was there. She hastened to open the door, so welcome was the sound of the well-known voice; but there, opposite to her, in the driving rain, rested the hurdle, with the confused mass lying huddled together upon it. The men who bore it were silent, standing with their faces turned toward her; all of them strangers, except the one neighbor, who was on her threshold.

"They found him lying out in the fields near the Woodhouse farm," said her neighbor, in a loud whisper; "he'd strayed there, we reckon."

"Is he dead?" she asked, mechanically.

"Not dead, bless your heart! no!" was the answer; "we'll carry him in. There now! Don't take on. There's a special providence over folks like him; they never come to much harm, you know. Show us where to lay him."

Ann Holland made way for the men to pass her, as they carried their burden into the quiet, pleasant kitchen. She followed with the light, and looked down upon him; her brother, who had played with her, and learned the same lessons, when they were innocent little children together. His gray hair was matted, and his bloated face smeared with dust and damp. He was barefooted and bareheaded. But as she gazed down upon him, and listened to his heavy struggle for breath, she cried in a tone of terror. "He is dying."

CHAPTER XI. LOST

An hour later the house was comparatively quiet again. A doctor had been, and said nothing could be done for Richard Holland, except to let him die where he was undisturbed. The men who had carried him home had dispersed, or had adjourned to the Upton Arms, to drink, and to talk over this close of a drunkard's life. The news had in some way reached the Rectory; and now only Mr. Chantrey and Ann Holland watched beside him. They had laid him, as he was, on the little white-covered sofa in the parlor, never so soiled before. Mr. Chantrey sat gazing at the degraded, dying man. No deeper debasement could come to any human being; almost the likeness of a human being had been lost. The mire and slough of the ditch into which he had fallen still clung to him; for only his face had been hastily washed clean by his sister's hand; a face that had forfeited all intelligence and seemliness; a coarse, squalid, disfigured face. Yet Ann was not repulsed by it; her tears fell upon it; and once she had bent over it, and kissed it gently. Now and then she put her mouth close to the deafened ear, and spoke to him, calling him by fond names, and imploring him to give some sign that he heard, and knew her. But there was no sign. The heavy breathing grew more thick and labored, yet feebler as the time passed slowly on. David Chantrey marvelled at the poor sister's patience and tenderness.

"Don't trouble to stay with me, sir," she said, at last, "I thought perhaps he'd come to himself, and you'd say a word to him. But there's no hope of that now."

"No," he answered, "I will not go, Ann," and his voice trembled with dread. "Do you think my wife could ever be as bad as this?"

"God forbid!" she cried, earnestly. "God keep her from it! Oh! if she could but see; if she could but know! But he wasn't always like this. He was a kind, good-natured, clever man once. It's drinking that's ruined him."

"I will stay with you to the end," said Mr. Chantrey; "it is fit for me. You are teaching me a lesson of patience, Ann. All this day I have been thinking if it would be possible for me to give up my wife, and send her away from me, to end her days apart from mine. I have been in despair; in the very deeps. But now; why! even if I knew she would die thus, I cannot forsake her."

"Ay! we must have patience," she answered. "I always hoped to win him back again, but it was too strong for him and me. God knows how he's been tempted on all hands; even those that call themselves religious, and go to church regular as can be. He used to cry to me sometimes, and promise to turn over a new leaf; and then somebody perhaps that he looked up to would treat him at the Upton Arms. He might have been a good man, if he'd been left alone."

"Let us pray together for him and ourselves," said Mr. Chantrey, kneeling down once again by the little couch, as he had knelt the night of his return home. Ann still held her brother's head upon her arm, and her bowed face nearly rested upon it. But all words failed David Chantrey. "Father!" he cried, "Father!" There was nothing more that he could say. It was the single, despairing call of a soul that was full of trouble; that was "laid in the lowest pit, in darkness, in the deeps." But the bewildered brain of the dying man caught the cry, and he muttered it over to himself; "Father! father! where is he?"

"It's God, our Father who art in heaven," said Ann Holland, uttering the words very slowly and distinctly in his ear; "try to think of Him, and pray to Him. He'll hear you, even now."

"Father!" he muttered again, "why! he'd be ashamed of his boy."

"It's God," she said, keeping down her sobs, "you've no other father. Think of Him: God, who loves you."

"He'd be ashamed of me," repeated the dying man.

For a minute or two he kept on whispering to himself words they could not hear, except the one word "shame." Then all was still. The miserable end had come; and neither love nor patience could avail him anything on this side the grave. He had gone as a drunkard into the presence of his Judge.

CHAPTER XII. A COLONIAL CURACY

The death of Richard Holland might have had a salutary effect upon Sophy Chantrey, if it had not been for the shock of learning how deeply she had disgraced herself and her husband in the sight of his people. She felt that she could never again face those who had seen her on that Sunday morning. She shut herself up in her room, refusing to admit any one, except the servant who waited upon her, and steadily set herself against any communication with the world outside. Even her husband she would hardly speak to; and her child she would not see. The strain and stress of her remorse was more than she could bear. Before the week was gone, she had fled for forgetfulness to the vice which bound her in so heavy a chain. All the cunning of her nature, so strangely perverted, was put into action to procure a supply of the stimulants she craved; and she escaped from her misery for a little while by losing herself in suicidal lethargy and stupefaction.

Mr. Chantrey himself felt it to be impossible to meet the gaze of his usual congregation; he shrank even from walking through the streets of his own town, while his shame was fresh upon him. He exchanged duties with fellow-clergymen, and so evaded the immediate difficulty. But he knew that this could not go on for long. He could not conscientiously retain a position such as he held, if he had not the moral and mental strength necessary for the discharge of its obligations. Strength of all kinds seemed to fail him. His physical vitality was low; the health he had gained in Madeira had been too severely taxed since his return. He had fought bravely against the mental feebleness that was creeping gradually over him with a paralyzing languor; but he knew he could not bear the conflict much longer. Everything was telling against him. He would fain have proved to his people that a man can live out a noble, useful, Christ-like life, under crushing sorrows, and shame that was worse than sorrow. But it was not in him to do it. He found himself feeble and crippled, in the very thick of life's battle; and it appeared to him that his position as rector of the parish rendered his feebleness tenfold disastrous.

But this decay of power came slowly, though surely. By the close of his second winter in England he felt within himself that he must quit his country again, if he wished to live only a few years longer. There had been no bright sunny spot of gladness for him, no gleam of hope throughout the whole winter. He had been compelled to send his boy away again to school, to shield him from seeing the disgrace of his mother. His friends had almost ceased to come to his house, and he had no heart to go to theirs. It was only now and then that he accepted his aunt's invitations to dine alone with her.

"Aunt," he said one evening, when they two were alone together in her fantastic drawing-room, "I have resigned my living."

Brought Home

"Resigned your living!" she repeated, in utter amazement, "resigned Upton Rectory!"

She could hardly pronounce the words; and she gazed at him with an air of bewilderment which brought a smile to his careworn face.

"Yes," he answered, "life has grown intolerable to me here."

"And what do you mean to do?" she asked.

"I am going out to my friend Warden," he replied, "who has a charge in New Zealand; he promises me a curacy under him, if I can get nothing better. But I am sure of a charge of my own very soon."

"A curate to Warden! a curate in New Zealand!" ejaculated Mrs. Bolton. "David, are you mad?"

"Not mad, but in most sober sadness," he said. "Life is impossible to me here, and under my circumstances; and I wish to live a few years longer for Sophy's sake, and my boy's. New Zealand is the very place for me."

"But you can go away again for a year or two," said his aunt, "and come back when your health is restored. The bishop will give you permission readily. You must not give up your living because your health fails."

"The bishop has my resignation, and my reasons for it," answered Mr. Chantrey, "and ho has accepted it kindly and regretfully, he says; but he fully approves of it. All there is to be done now is to sell our household goods, and sail for a new home, in a new world."

"And Sophy?" gasped Mrs. Bolton; "what do you mean to do with her? Where shall you leave her?"

"She must come with me," he said; "I shall never leave her again. It will be a new chance for her: and with God's help she may yet conquer. Even if she cannot, it will be easier for me to bear my burden among strangers than here, where every one knows all about us. A missionary curate in New Zealand will be a very different personage from the rector of Upton."

Brought Home

He looked at his aunt with a smile, and an expression of hope, such as had not lit up his gray face for many a month. This new life opening before him, with all its social disadvantages, and many privations, would give his wife such an opportunity for recovery as the conventionalities of society at home could not furnish. Hope had visited him again, and he cherished it as a most welcome visitant.

"Good Heavens!" cried Mrs. Bolton, lost in astonishment, "David, you must not throw yourself away in this manner! I will see the bishop myself, and recall to his memory his old friendship for the archdeacon. He cannot have promised the living yet to any one. What would become of me, here in Upton, settled as I am, with a stranger in the rectory? Why did you not ask my advice before taking such a rash step?"

"Because I should not have followed your advice," he answered. "I settled the whole matter in my own mind before I broached it even to Warden. It is the only chance for us both. I am a broken, defeated man."

"Oh, my boy!" she exclaimed, with tears in her eyes, "I cannot consent to your going away. You have always been my favorite nephew; and I could not endure to see a stranger in your place. It is all Sophy's fault. And why should you sacrifice your life, and Charlie's, for her? Let some place at a distance be found for her; no one will blame you, and you will not suffer so much from the disgrace, if you do not witness it. Only stay in Upton, and all I have shall be yours. It will be a happy place to you again, if you will only wait patiently for brighter days."

"No," he said, sorrowfully; "it has been a pleasant place to me, but it can never be so again. I must go for Sophy's sake. There is no hope for her here; there is hope for her among new scenes and fresh influences. I have spoken to her about it, and she is eager to go; she feels that there would be a chance for her. To turn away from my purpose now would be to doom her to her sin without hope of deliverance. It would be impossible for me to do that."

It was a terrible blow to Mrs. Bolton. She foresaw endless mortifications and heartburnings for herself in the presence, and under the rule, of a strange rector at Upton, over whom she would have no more authority or influence than any other parishioner. Besides, she was really fond of her nephew, and anxious to make his life smooth and agreeable to him. No one could be blind to the fact that his health was giving way again, and she thought with some apprehension of the life of hardship and poverty he was choosing. That he should throw away all that was desirable and advantageous for the sake of his wife, who was merely a trouble and dishonor to him, was an infatuation that she could not understand. He pointed out to her that he was also losing his influence over his people, and she maintained that even this was no reason why he should give up a suitable living and a pleasant rectory. At last, angry with him, and apprehensive for her future position in the parish, she refused to listen any longer to his representations, and spent the few weeks that intervened before their departure in a state of offended estrangement.

CHAPTER XIII. SELF-SACRIFICE

All Upton was thrown into a ferment by the unexpected news that their rector had resigned his living, and was about to emigrate to New Zealand. At first it was declared too strange to be true. Then in a few of the lower class taverns it was said to be too good to be true; but in the Upton Arms, where the landlady considered it her duty to be regular at church, and even the landlord thought it the thing to go there pretty often, a civil amount of regret was expressed. It was the fault of his wife, said most of the respectable parishioners, who unfortunately did not know when she had had enough of a good thing. Even those who were in the same plight with herself threw a stone at poor Sophy when they heard that their pleasant-spoken, affable, popular rector, as he used to be, was about to flee his country. Very few sympathized with him. He was taking an unheard-of, preposterous, fanatical course. How could a man in his senses give up a living of L400 a year, with a pretty rectory and glebe-land, for a colonial curacy?

But there was one person who heard the news, and brooded over it silently, with very different feelings. The last few months had been very tranquil ones for Ann Holland. The one anxiety of her quiet life had been removed, and after the first sorrow was passed she had found her home a very peaceful place without her brother. Her old neighbors could come in now to take tea with her without any dread of being rudely disturbed. The business did not suffer; it was rather increasing, and she had had some thoughts of employing a second journeyman. But to hear that Mr. Chantrey was going to leave Upton, and that very soon she should see neither him nor Charlie, who made her house so merry whenever he ran in, was as great a blow to her as to Mrs. Bolton.

Ann Holland had been born in the house she lived in, and had never dwelt anywhere else.

Brought Home

All her world lay within the compass of a few miles from it, among the farm-houses where her business or her early friendships had made her acquainted with the inhabitants. The people of Upton only were her fellow-countrymen; all others were foreigners, and to her, lawful objects of mistrust. Every other land save her own seemed a strange and perilous place. Of New Zealand she had not even any vague ideas, for it was nothing but a name to her. She had far clearer views of heaven, of that other world into which she had seen so many of her childhood's friends pass away. To lie down upon her bed and die would have been a familiar journey to her compared with that strange voyage across boundless seas to a country of which she knew nothing but the name.

Yet they were going—Mr. Chantrey, with his failing health; Mrs. Chantrey, a victim to a miserable vice; and Charlie, the young, inexperienced boy. What a helpless set! She tried to picture them passing through the discomforts and dangers of a savage life, as she supposed it to be; Mr. Chantrey ill, poor, friendless, and homeless. Upon her screen were the announcements of his coming to the living, of his marriage, the birth of both children, and the death of one. She read them over word for word, with eyes fast filling and growing dim with tears. Very soon there would be another column in the newspaper telling of his resignation and departure—perhaps shortly afterward of his death. He would die in that far-off country, with no one to care for him or nurse him except his unhappy wife. She could not bear to think of it. She must go with them.

But how could she ever bear to quit Upton? All her own people were buried in the churchyard there, and she kept their graves green with turf, and their headstones free from moss. She had no memories or associations anywhere else, and she clung to all such memories and cherished them fondly. There was no one in Upton who knew the pedigrees of every family as she did. Even her household goods, old and quaint as they were, had a halo from the light of other days about them. How many persons, dead and gone now, had she seen sit opposite to her in that old arm-chair! How often had childish faces looked laughingly at themselves in her pewter plates? Her mother's chairs and sofa, worked in tent-stitch, which only saw the daylight twice a year—what would become of them, and what common uses would they be put to in any other house? Her heart failed her when she thought of leaving these things. It was not, moreover, simply leaving them, as she would have to do when she died, but she must see them sold and scattered before her eyes, and behold the vacant places empty and forlorn, without their old belongings. Could she bear to be so uprooted?

Brought Home

"Sir," she said one evening, when Mr. Chantrey, worn out with the conflict of his own parting with his people, was sitting depressed and silent by her fireside, "Mr. Chantrey, are you thinking of taking out a servant with you?"

"No," he answered; "the cost would be too much. You forget we are going to be poor folks out yonder, Ann. Don't you remember telling me it might have been better for my wife if she had had to work hard for Charlie and me?"

"That was long ago," she replied; "it's different now. Who's to mind you if you are ill? and who's to see Master Charlie kept nice, like a gentleman's son? I've been thinking it would break my heart to sit at home thinking of you all. There is nothing to keep me here, now my poor brother's gone. Take me with you, sir."

"No, no!" he exclaimed, vehemently—so vehemently that she knew how his heart leaped at the thought of it; "you must not sacrifice yourself for us. What! give up this pleasant home of yours, and all your old friends?! No; it cannot be."

"There'd be trouble in it," she said; "but it would be a harder trouble to think of you in foreign parts, with none but savages about you, and no roof over your head, and wild beasts marauding about."

"Not so bad as that," he interrupted, smiling so cheerfully that her own face brightened. "There are no wild beasts, and not many natives, and I shall have a home of my own somewhere."

"I could never sleep at nights," she went on, "or eat my bread in comfort, for wondering about you. I don't want to be a cost to you; and when I've sold all, I shall have a little sum of money in hand that will keep me a year or two after my passage is paid. I'm not too old for work yet. If it's too bad a place for me to go to, what must it be for you? And you're not as strong as you ought to be, sir. If anything should happen to you out there, you'd like to know I was with them you love, taking care of them."

"It would be a greater comfort than I can tell," said Mr. Chantrey, in a tremulous voice. "Now and then the thought crosses my mind that I might die yonder; and what would become of Sophy and Charlie, left so desolate? There's Warden; but he is too austere and harsh, good as he is. But, Ann, I ought not to let you come."

Brought Home

"There's no duty to keep me at home," she answered. "If my poor brother was alive, I could never forsake him, you know; but that is all over now. And I could have patience with her, poor lady! Aye, I'd have patience for her own sake as well as yours. She could never try me as I've been tried. And I've great hopes of her. Maybe if James, poor fellow, could have broken off all his old ways, and begun again fresh, turning over a new leaf where folks hadn't seen the old one, he might have been saved. I've great hopes of Mrs. Chantrey; and nobody could help her as I could. It seems almost as if our blessed Lord laid this thing before me, and asked me to do it for his sake. Sure if he asked me to go all round the world for him, I couldn't say no. To go to New Zealand with folks I love will be nothing to him leaving heaven, with his Father and the holy angels there, to live and work like a poor man in this world, and to die on the cross at the end of all."

Her voice fell into its lowest and tenderest key as she spoke these last words, and the tears stood in her eyes, as if the thought of Christ's life, so long familiar, had started into a new meaning for her. The opportunity for copying Him more literally than she had ever done before was granted to her, and her spirit sprang forward eagerly to seize it. Mr. Chantrey sat silent, yet with a lighter heart than he had had for months. He felt that if Ann Holland went out with them half his load would be gone. There was a brighter hope for Sophy, and there would be a sure friend for his boy, whatever his own fate might be. Yet he shrank from accepting such a sacrifice, and could only see the selfishness of doing so at the first moment.

"You must take another week to think of it," he said.

But when the week was ended Ann Holland was more confirmed in her wish than before. The news that she was going out with Mr. Chantrey's family caused as great a stir in the town as that of the rector's resignation. The Hollands had always been saddlers in Upton, and all the true old Upton people had faithfully adhered to them, never being tempted away by interlopers from London or other places, who professed to do better work at lower prices. To be sure the last male Holland was gone, but every one knew that his only share in the business for many years had been the spending of the money it brought in. That Ann Holland should give up her good trade and go out as servant to the Chantreys—for so it was represented by the news-bearers—was an unheard-of, incredible thing. Many were the remonstrances she had to listen to, and to answer as best she could.

It was a bitter day for Ann Holland when she saw her treasured household furniture sold by auction and scattered to the four winds. Many of her old neighbors bought for themselves some mementoes of the place they knew so well, but the bulk of the larger articles were sold without sentiment or feeling. It was a pang to part with each one of them, as they were carried off to some strange or hostile house to be put to common uses. The bare walls and empty rooms that were left, which she had never seen bare and empty before, seemed terribly new, yet familiar to her. She wandered through them for a few minutes, loitering in each one as she thought of all that had happened to her during her monotonous life; and then, with a sorrowful yet brave heart, she walked along the street to the rectory, which was already dismantled and bare like the home she had just left.

CHAPTER XIV. FAREWELLS

During these busy weeks Mrs. Bolton had looked on in almost sullen silence, except when now and then she had broken out into a passionate invective of her nephew's madness. He had never been indifferent to the luxuries and refinements that give a charm to life, and her nature could not comprehend how all these were poisoned at their source for him. He was eager to exchange them for a chance of a true home, however lowly that home might be. He would willingly have gone to the wilds of Siberia, if by so doing he could secure his wife's reformation An almost feverish haste possessed him. To carry her away from Upton, from England, and to enter upon a quite new career in a strange place, and to accomplish this plan quickly, absorbed him nearly to the exclusion of any other thought. Mrs. Bolton felt herself very much neglected and greatly aggrieved. Her plans were frustrated and her comforts threatened, yet her nephew hardly seemed to think of her—he for whom she had done so much, who would not have been even rector of Upton but for the late archdeacon.

Yet she relented a little from her displeasure as the day for parting came. She was as fond of him and his boy as her nature would allow. Sophy had never been otherwise than an object of her jealousy, and now she positively detested her. But when Mr. Chantrey came on the last evening to sit an hour or two with her, and she saw, as with newly-opened eyes, his care-worn face and wearied, feeble frame, her heart quite melted toward him.

"Remember," she said, eagerly, "you can come back again whenever yon choose, as soon as you grow sure how useless this mad scheme is. I wish I could have persuaded you to keep on your living, but yon are too wilful. You are welcome to draw upon me for funds to return at any time, and I shall supply them gladly, and give you a home here. If yon find your expectations fail, promise me to come back."

"And bring Sophy with me?" he asked, with almost a smile.

"No, no," she answered, shrinking involuntarily from the idea of having her in her house. "Oh, my poor boy! what can yon do?"

"I can only bear the burden sin lays upon me," he said. "It is not permitted to us to shake off the iniquities of others. All of us, more or less, must share in the sufferings of Christ, bearing our portion of the sins of the world, which he bore, even unto death. I am ready to die, if that will save my poor Sophy from her sin.

"But all that makes a Christian life so miserable!" exclaimed Mrs. Bolton.

"If in this life only we have hope in Christ, then are we of all men most miserable," he answered.

"And you would teach that we must give up everything," she cried, "all advantages, and blessings, and innocent indulgences, and pleasures of every kind?"

"If the sins or temptations of those about call for such a sacrifice, we must give them up, every one," he replied; "they are no longer blessings or innocent indulgences. If God calls upon us to make some sacrifice, and we refuse to do it, do you think he will yield like some weak parent, who will suffer his child to run the risk of serious injury rather than give him present pain? The whole law of our life is sacrifice, as it was the law of Christ's life. It is possible that some small self-denial at the right moment may spare us some costly expiation later on. Christianity must perish if it loses sight of this law."

Mrs. Bolton did not answer him. Was he thinking of her own refusal to remove temptation out of the way of his wife when she first began to fall into her fatal habit? He was not in reality thinking of her at all, but her conscience pricked her, though her pride kept her silent. It was such an unheard-of course for a person in her station, that none but fanatics could expect her to take it. Quixotic, irrational, eccentric, visionary, were words that flitted incoherently through her brain; but her tongue refused to utter them. Was

Brought Home

Christ then so prudent, so cautious, so anxious to secure innocent indulgences and to grasp worldly advantages? Could she think of Him making life easy and comfortable to Himself while hundreds of thousands, nay, millions of unhappy souls were hurrying each year into misery and ruin?

There was not much conversation between her and her nephew; for as a parting draws very near, our memories refuse to serve us, and we forget to say the many, many things we may perhaps never again have any season for saying. They bade one another farewell tenderly and sorrowfully; and he went out, under the tranquil, starry sky, to wander once more beside the grave of his little child, and under the old gray walls of his church. He had not known till now how hard the trial would be. Up to this time he had been kept incessantly occupied with the numberless arrangements necessary for so great a change; but these were all completed. He had said farewell to his people; but the aching of his own great personal grief and shame had prevented him from feeling that separation too forcibly. But the stir and excitement were over for the hour. Here there were no cold, curious eyes fastened upon him; no fear of any harsh voice putting into words of untimely lamentation the unacknowledged reason of his departure. The beloved familiar places, so quiet yet so full of associations to him, had full power over his spirit; and he could not resist them. The very ivy-leaves rustling against the tower, and the low, sleepy chirp of the little birds disturbed by his tread, were dear to him. What, then, was the church itself, every lineament of which he knew as well as if they were the features of a friend? It was a beautiful old church; but if it had been the homeliest and barest building ever erected, he must still have mourned over the pulpit, where he had taught his people; the pews, where their listening faces were lifted up to him; the little vestry, where he had spent so many peaceful hours. And the small mound, blooming with flowers, under which his child slept, how much power had that over him! He paced restlessly up and down beneath the solemn yew-trees, his heart breaking over them all. To-morrow by this time he would have left them far behind him; and never more would his eyes behold them, or his feet tread the path he had so often trod. They seemed to cry to him like living, sentient things. To and fro he wandered, while the silent stars and the waning moon, lying low in the sky above the church, looked down upon him with a pale and mournful light. At last the morning came; and he remembered that to-day he must quit them all, and sail for a far-off country.

The vessel Mr. Chantrey had chosen for the long voyage was a merchant ship, sailing for Melbourne, under a captain who had been an early friend of his own, and who knew the reason for his leaving England. No other cabin passengers had taken berths on board her, though there were a few emigrants in the steerage. Captain Scott, himself a water-drinker, had arranged that no intoxicating beverages, in any form, should appear in the saloon. The steward was strictly forbidden to supply them to any person except Mr. Chantrey himself. This enforced abstinence, the complete change of scene, and the fresh sea-breezes during the protracted voyage, he reckoned upon as the best means of restoring his wife to health of body and mind. Ann Holland, too, would watch over her as vigilantly and patiently as himself; and Charlie would be always at hand to amuse her with his boyish chatter. A bright hope was already dawning upon him.

CHAPTER XV. IN DESPAIR

It was early in June when they set sail; and as the vessel floated down the Channel somewhat slowly against the western wind Ann Holland spent most of her time on deck, watching, often with dim eyes, the coasts of England, as they glided past her. She could still hardly realize the change that had torn her so completely away from her old life. It made her brain swim to think of Upton, and the old neighbors going about the streets on their daily business, and the church-clock striking out the hours; and the sun rising and setting, and the days passing by, and she not there. It felt all a dream to her; an odd, inexplicable, endless dream, which never could become as real as the old days had been. Her thoughts were all busy with the past, recalling faces and events long ago forgotten; she scarcely ever looked on to the end of the voyage. The sea was calm, and the soft wind sang low among the rigging, while point after point along the shores stole by, and were lost to sight almost unheeded, though she could not turn her steadfast, sorrowful gaze from them till she could see them no more. Yet when Mr. Chantrey, reproaching himself for bringing her, asked her if she repented, she was always ready to say heartily that she would not go back, and leave them, for the world.

Charlie alone of them all was quite happy in the change. For the last nine months he had been constantly at school; seldom going home, and then but for a day or two, when his mother was at her best. The boy found himself all at once set free from school restraints, restored to his father and mother, who had no one else to interest them; and with all the delights of a ship and a voyage added to his other joys. He was wild with happiness. There was not one thing left him to wish for; for even his mother's nervous state of health could not cast any gloom upon his gladness. He had grown accustomed to think of her as

Brought Home

a confirmed invalid; and when she came on deck he would sit quietly beside her for a little while, and lower his clear young voice in speaking to her, without feeling that his short-lived self-control damped his pleasure. But she was not often there long enough to test his devotion too greatly.

Sophy Chantrey was passing through a season of intense misery, both of mind and body; more bitter even than the wretchedness she had felt when she could indulge the craving that had taken so deep a hold upon her. There was nothing voluntary in her abstinence, and consequently neither pleasure nor pride in being able to exercise self-command. Her health was greatly enfeebled; and her mind had been weakened almost to childishness. She felt as if her husband was treating her cruelly; yet she could see keenly that it was she who had brought ruin upon his future prospects, as well as those of her boy. She had never been able to sink into utter indifference; and she could not forget, strive as she would, all the happy past, and the unutterably wretched present. Here, on board ship, there was no chance for her to procure the narcotics, with which she had lulled her self-reproaches formerly. Her longing for such stimulants amounted almost to delirium. She could not sleep for want of them; and all day long she thought of them, and cried for them, until her husband and Ann Holland could scarcely persevere in refusing them to her. It seemed to them at times as if she must lose her reason, the little that remained to her, and become insane, unless they yielded to her vehement entreaties. Even when, after the first week was gone, and the craving was in some measure deadened, her spirits did not rally. She would lie still on deck when her husband carried her there, or on the narrow berth in their cabin, with eyes closed, and hands listlessly folded, an image of despair.

"Sophy!" he cried one day, when she had not stirred, or raised her eyelids for hours; "Sophy, do you wish to kill me?"

"I have killed you," she muttered, still without moving, or looking at him.

"Sophy," he answered, "you are dreaming Look up, and see me here alive, beside you Life lies before us yet; for you and me together."

"No" she said, "don't I know it is death to you to be tied to me as you are? I am a curse to you, and you hate and loathe me, as I do myself. But we cannot get rid of each other, you and me. Oh! if I could but die, and set you free!"

Brought Home

"I do not hate you," he answered, tenderly; "you are still very dear to me. I do not wish to be free from you."

"Then you ought," she cried, with sudden passion; "you ought to hate that which degrades and shames you. I am dragging you down to ruin; you and Charlie. Do you think I do not know it? Oh! if I could but die. Perhaps I may live for many, many years yet; live to be an old woman, a drunken old wretch! Think what it will be to live for years and years with a lost creature like me. It is death, and worse than death, for you."

"But why should you be lost?" he asked; "have you never thought of One who came to seek and to save that which is lost?"

"Yes; He found me once," she said, in tones of despair, "He found me once; but I strayed away again, wilfully, in spite of His love, and all He had done for me. I knew what He had done, and how He loved me; yet I went away from Him wilfully. I chose ruin; and now He leaves me to my choice."

"This is the delusion of a sick brain," he answered; "you have no power to think rightly of our Lord. Listen to what I can tell you about Him, and His love for you."

"No," she interrupted; "none of you others know, you people who have never fallen like me. You do not know what it is to feel yourselves given up and sold to sin. You and Ann Holland think you can save me by keeping temptation out of my way; but I know that as soon as it comes again I shall be as weak as water against it."

"Have you no wish to be saved, then?" he asked, his heart sinking within him at her hopeless words.

"Wish to be saved!" she repeated; "did the rich man in torments wish to be saved? He only asked for one drop of water to cool his tongue but for a moment. He knew he could not be saved, and he did not pray for it."

"Do you think that I have no wish for your salvation?" he asked. "Am I leaving you in your sin? Have I done nothing, given up nothing, to secure it? Has Ann Holland given up nothing?"

Brought Home

"Oh! you have," she cried. "You are doing all you can for me, but it is useless."

"Christ has done more," he said. "His love for you passes ours infinitely. Then if you have not wearied out ours, can you possibly exhaust his? He can stoop to you in all your misery and sinfulness, if you will but stretch out your hand toward Him. There is no sin He will not forgive, and none He cannot conquer, if you will but rouse yourself to work with Him. Against your own will He cannot save you."

"I will try," she murmured.

Yet time after time the same subject, almost in the same words, was renewed. Sophy's enfeebled brain could not long retain the thought of a divine love and power, which was ceaselessly though secretly striving to reclaim her. There was no opportunity for her to exert her own will, for she could not be tempted in her present circumstances, and the strength gained by such an exertion was impossible to her. Again and again, with untiring patience, did Mr. Chantrey give ear to her despairing utterances, and meet them with soothing arguments. But often he felt himself on the verge of despair, doubtful of the truths he was trying so earnestly to implant again in her heart. In the smooth happy days of old, both of them had believed them. But now he asked himself, Does God indeed care? Does He see and know? Is He near at hand, and not afar off?

Their vessel had entered the tropical seas, and a profound unbroken monotony reigned around them. They had not sighted land since the shores of England had sunk below the horizon. A waste of waters encircled them, and a dead calm prevailed. Through the sultry and hazy atmosphere no rain fell in cooling showers. Day after day the sea was of perfect stillness, and an oppressive silence, as of death, brooded over the low, regular heaving of the waters. The dry torrid heat was exhausting, and the ship with its idle sails made but little way across the quiet sea. Mr. Chantrey's weakened frame suffered greatly, and even Ann Holland's brave and cheery spirit almost sank into despondency.

"If it hadn't been for Mrs. Chantrey," she thought mournfully, "we should all have been at Upton now, as happy as the day's long. The summer's at its height there, and the harvest is being gathered in. How cool it would be under the chestnut-trees, or under the church walls! Mr. Chantrey's sinking, plain enough, and what is to become of us if he should die before we get to that foreign land? Dear, dear! whoever would go to sea if they could get only a place to lay their heads on land?"

CHAPTER XVI. A LONG VOYAGE

It was a dreary and monotonous time. After the sun had gone down, red and sullen, through the haze, and when the ship left a long track of phosphorescent light sparkling behind it, Mr. Chantrey would pace up and down the deck, as he had often walked to and fro in the churchyard paths in the starlight. He had many things to think of. For his wife his hope was strengthening; a dim star shone before him in the future. Her brain was gradually regaining clearness, and her mind strength. Something of the old buoyancy and elasticity was returning to her, for she would play sometimes with her child merrily, and her laugh was like music to him. But how would it be in the hour of temptation, which must come? She said her craving for stimulants was passing away; but how would she bear being again able to procure them? He would watch over her and guard her as long as he lived, but what would become of her if he should die?

This last question was becoming every day more and more urgent. The exhausting oppressive heat and the protracted voyage were sapping his strength, and he knew it. The fresh sweet sea-breezes on which he had reckoned had failed him, and he was consciously nearer death than when he left England. He longed eagerly for life and health, that he might see his wife and child in happier circumstances before he died. To leave them thus seemed intolerable to him. What was he to do with his boy? He could not leave him in the care of a mother not yet delivered from the bondage of such a fatal sin. Yet to separate him harshly from her would almost certainly doom her to continue in it. If life might be spared to him only a few years longer, he would probably see her once more a fitting guardian for their child. The growing hope for her, the dim dread for himself—these two held alternate sway over him as he paced to and fro under the southern skies.

Captain Scott, his friend, urged upon him that there was one remedy open to him, and only one on board the ship. The long stress and strain upon his physical as well as his mental health had weakened him until his strength was slowly ebbing away; his heart beat feebly, and his whole system had fallen under a nervous depression. Now was the time when, as a medicine, the alcohol, which was poison and death to his wife, would prove restoration to him. Could he but keep up his vital powers until the voyage was ended, all would be well with him. His life might be prolonged for those few years he so ardently desired. He could still watch over his wife, and protect his child during boyhood,

Brought Home

and die in peace—young perhaps, but having accomplished what he had set his mind upon. But Sophy? How could she bear this unexpected temptation? He did not suppose he could effectually conceal it from her, for of late she had clung to him like a child, following him about humbly and meekly, with a touching dependence upon him, striving to catch his eye and to smile faintly when he looked at her, as a child might do who was seeking to win forgiveness. She was very feeble and delicate still, her appetite was as dainty as his own, and the heat oppressed her almost as much as himself. Yet that which might save him would certainly destroy her.

Day after day the debate with Captain Scott was resumed. But there was no real debate in his own mind. He would gladly take the remedy if he could do so with safety to his wife, but not for a thousand lives would he endanger her soul. Not for the certainty of prolonging his own years would he take from her the merest chance of overcoming her sin. To do it for an uncertainty was impossible.

There was hope for him still, if the vessel could but get past these sultry seas into a cooler climate. One good fresh sea-breeze would do him more good than any stimulant, and they were slowly gliding to latitudes where they might meet them at any hour. Once out of the tropics, and around the Cape of Good Hope, there would be no fear of exhausting heat in the air they breathed. All his languor would be gone and the rest of the voyage would bring health and vigor to his fevered frame. Only let them double the Cape, and a new life in a new world lay before them.

His brain felt confused and delirious at times, but he knew it so well that he grew used to sit down silently in the bow of the ship, and let the dizzy dreams pass over him, careful not to alarm his wife or Ann Holland. Cool visions of the pleasant English home he had quitted for ever; the shadows and the calm of his church, where the sunshine slanted in through narrow windows made green with ivy-leaves; the rustling of leaves in the elm-trees on his lawn in the soft low wind of a summer's evening; the deep grassy glades of thick woods, where he had loved to walk; the murmuring and tinkling of hidden brooks—all these flitted across his clouded mind as he sat speechless, with his throbbing head resting upon his hands. Often his wife crouched beside him, herself silent, thinking sadly how he was brooding over all the wrong and injury she had done him, yet fearing in her humiliation to ask him if it were so. Her repentance was very deep and real, her love for him very true. Yet she dreaded the hour when she must face temptation again. She could not even bear to think of it.

But shortly after they had passed the southern tropic, as they neared the Cape, the climate changed suddenly, with so swift an alteration that from sultry heat of a torrid summer they plunged almost directly into the biting cold of winter. As they doubled the Cape a strong north−west gale met them, with icy cold in its blast. The ropes were frozen, and the sails grew stiff with hoar−frost. Rough seas rolled about them, tossing the vessel like a toy upon their waves. The change was too sudden and too great. All the passengers were ill, and David Chantrey lay down in his low, narrow berth, knowing well that no hope was left to him.

CHAPTER XVII. ALMOST SHIPWRECKED

Sophy Chantrey was left alone to nurse her dying husband, for Ann Holland was lying ill in her own cabin, ignorant of his extremity. Captain Scott came down for a minute or two, but he could not stay beside him. His presence was sorely needed on deck, yet he lingered awhile, looking sorrowfully at his friend. Sophy watched him with a clearer and keener glance in her blue eyes than he had ever yet seen in them.

"What is the matter with him?" she asked, following him to the cabin door.

"As near dying as possible," he answered, gruffly. He believed that a good life had been sacrificed to a bad one, and he could not bring himself to speak softly to the woman who was the cause of it.

"Dying!" she cried. There was no color to fade from her face, but the light died from her eyes, and the word faltered on her lips.

"Yes," he answered, "dying."

"Sophy, come to me," called her husband, in feeble tones.

She left the captain, and returned at once to his side. The low berth was almost on the floor, and she had to kneel to bring her face nearer to his. It was night, and the only light was the dim glimmer of an oil−lamp, which the captain had hung to the ceiling, and which swung to and fro with the lurching of the ship. The wind was whistling shrilly among the rigging, and every plank and board in the vessel groaned and creaked under the beating of the waves. Now and then her feet were ankle–deep in water, and she dreaded to see it sweep over the low berth. In the rare intervals of the storm she could hear the hurried movements overhead, and the shouts of the sailors as they called to one another from the rigging. But vaguely she heard, and saw, and felt. Her husband's face, white and haggard and thin, with his gray hair and his eyes sunken with unshed tears, was all that she could distinctly realize.

"Sophy," he said, "do not leave me again."

He held out his hand, and she laid hers into it, shuddering as she felt its chilly grasp. Her head fell on to the pillow beside his, and her lips, close to his ear, spoke to him through sobs.

"Is there nothing that can be done?" she cried. "It is I who have killed you. Must you really die for my sin, and leave us?"

"I think I must die," he said, touching her head softly with his feeble hand. "I would live for you if I could—for you and my poor boy. Sophy, promise me while I can hear you, while you can speak to me, promise me you will never fall into this sin again."

"How can I?" she cried. "I have killed you, and now who will care?"

"God will care," he said, faintly, "and I shall care; wherever I may be I shall care. Promise me, my darling, my poor girl!"

"I promise you," she answered, with a deep sob.

"You will never let yourself enter into temptation?"

"Never!" she cried.

"Never taste it; never look at it; never think of it, if possible. Promise," he whispered again.

"Never!" she sobbed; "never! Oh, live, and you shall see me conquer. God will help me to conquer, and you will help me. Do not leave us. O God, do not let him die!"

Brought Home

But he did not hear her. A faintness and numbness that seemed like death, which had been creeping languidly through his veins for some time, darkened his eyes and sealed his lips. He could not see her, and her voice sounded far away. She called again and again upon him, but there was no answer. The deep roar of the storm on the other side of the frail wooden walls thundered continuously, and the groan of the straining planks grated upon her ear as she listened intently for one or more word from him. Was she then alone with him, dying? Was there no help, nothing that could be at least attempted for his help? Through the uproar and tumult she caught the sound of some one stirring in the saloon. She sprang to the door, and met Captain Scott on the point of opening it.

"Come," said she frantic with terror; "he is dead already."

The captain bent over the dying man, and with the promptitude of one to whom time was of the utmost value passed his hand rapidly over his benumbed and paralyzed body.

"No, not dead," he exclaimed; "but he's sinking fast, and there's only one remedy. You can leave him to die, or you can save him, Mrs. Chantrey. There is no one else to nurse him, and every moment is precious to me. Here's a brandy–flask. Give him some at once; force a few drops through his teeth, and watch the effect it has upon him. As he swallows it give him a little more every few minutes. Watch him carefully; it will be life or death with him. If I can get down again I'll come in to see you, but I am badly wanted on deck this moment. There's enough there, but not too much, remember. Get him warm, if possible. God bless you, Mrs. Chantrey."

He had been busily heaping rugs and blankets upon his friend's insensible form; and now, with a hearty grasp of the hand, and an earnest glance into her face, he hurried away, leaving Sophy alone once more.

A shudder of terror ran through her, and she called to him not to leave her; but he did not hear. She stood in the middle of the cabin, looking around as if for help, but there was none. The craving, which had been starved within her by the forced abstinence of the last few weeks, awoke again with insufferable fierceness. She was cold herself, chilled to the very heart; her misery of body and soul were extreme. The dim light and the ceaseless roar of the storm oppressed her. The very scent of the brandy seemed to intoxicate her, and steal away her resolution. If she took but a very little of it, she reasoned with herself, she would be better fitted for the long, exhausting task of watching her husband. How would she have strength to stand over him through the cold, dark hours of the night, feeble and worn out as she already felt herself? For his sake, then, she must taste it; she would take but a very little. The captain had said there was not more than enough; but surely he would give her more, to save her husband's life. Only a little, just to stay the intolerable craving.

Sophy poured out a small, portion into the little horn belonging to the flask. The strong spirituous scent excited her. How warm, and strong, and useful it would make her to her husband in his extremity! Yet still she hesitated. Suppose she could not resist the temptation to take more, and yet more, until she lost her consciousness, and left him to perish with cold and faintness? She knew how often she had resolved to take but a taste, enough to drive away the painful dejection of the passing hour; and how fatally her resolution had failed her, when once she had yielded. If she should fail now, if the temptation conquered her, there was no shadow of a hope for him. When she came to her senses again he would be dead.

Why did not somebody come to her help? Where was Ann Holland, that she should be away just at the very moment when her presence was most desirable and most necessary? How could Captain Scott think of trusting her with poison? How could she do battle with so close and subtle a tempter? So long a battle, too; though all the dreary hours of the storm! Only a little while ago she had made a solemn promise never to fall into this sin, never to enter into temptation. But she had been thrust into temptation unawares, in an instant, with no one to help her, and no time to gather strength for resistance. Even David himself could not blame her if she broke her promise. It should be only a taste; it could not be more than that, for the flask was not full; and now she came to think of it she could not get on deck to ask the captain for more, because the hatches were closed. That would save her from taking too much. She would keep the thought before her that every drop she swallowed was taken from her dying husband, for whom there was barely enough. She could only taste it, and she did it for his sake, not her own.

She lifted the little horn to her lips; but before tasting the stimulant, she glanced round, as she had often done before, to see if any one was looking at her; a stealthy cunning movement, born of the sense of shame she had never quite lost. Every nerve was quivering with excitement, and her heart was beating quickly. But her glance fell upon her husband's face turned toward her, yet with no watchful, reproachful eyes fastened upon her. The eyelids half closed; the pallid, hollow cheeks; the head fallen back upon the pillow, looked like death. Was he then gone from her already? Had she suffered his flickering life to die out altogether, while she had been dallying with temptation? With a wild and very bitter cry Sophy Chantrey sprang to his side, and forced a few drops of the eau–de–vie between his clenched teeth. Again and again, patiently, she repeated her efforts, watching eagerly for the least sign of returning animation. Every thought of herself was gone now; she became absorbed between alternate hope and dread. He was alive still; slowly the death–like pallor was passing away, faint tokens of returning circulation tingled through his benumbed veins. The beating of his heart was stronger, and his hands seemed less icily cold. But so slowly, and with so many intermissions, did the change creep on, that she did not dare to assure herself that he was reviving. Now and then the scent made her feel sick with terror; for she knew that his life depended upon her unceasing attention, and the tempter was still beside her, though thrust back for the time by her newly–awakened will. "I will not let him die!" she cried to herself; yet she was inwardly fearful of failing in her resolution, and leaving him to die. Would the daylight never come? Would the storm never cease?

It was raging more wildly than ever; and Captain Scott found it impossible to go below, even though his friend was probably dying. Sophy was left absolutely alone. It seemed to her like an eternity, as she knelt beside her husband, desperately, fighting against sin, and intently watching for some sure sign of life in him. He was not dead, that was almost all she knew. The night was dark still, and very lonely. There was no one who saw her, none to care for her; and her misery was very great.

Was there none who cared? A still small voice in her own soul, long unheard, but speaking clearly through the din of the storm around and within her, asked, "Does not Christ care? He who came to seek and to save that which was lost? He whom God sent into the world to be the Captain of salvation, and to suffer being tempted, that He might be able to succor all those who are tempted?" For a moment she listened breathlessly as if some new thing had been said to her. Christ really cared for her; really knew her extremity in this dire temptation; was ready with His help, if she would but have it. Could it be true? If He were beside her, witnessing her temptation and her struggling, seeing and entering into all the bitterness of the passing hours, why! then such a presence and such a sympathy were a thousand times greater and better than if all the world beside had been by to cheer her. Why had she never realized this before? He knew; God knew; she was not alone, because the Father Himself was with her.

She had no time to pray consciously, in so many words of set speech; but her whole heart was full of prayer and hope. The terror of temptation was gone; nay, for the time, the temptation itself was gone, for she was lifted up far above it. She could use the powerful remedy on which her husband's life depended with no danger to herself. Her thoughts ran busily forward into a blissful future. How happy they would all be again! How diligently she would guard herself! Her life henceforth should be spent as under the eye of God.

At last the morning dawned, and a gray light stole even through the darkened portholes—a faint light, but sufficient for her to see her husband's face more clearly. His heart beat under her hand with more vigor, and the color had come back to his lips. She could see now how every drop he swallowed brought, a more healthy hue to his face. He had attempted to speak more than once, but she laid her hand on his mouth to enforce silence until his strength was more equal to the effort. At last he whispered earnestly that she could not refuse to listen.

"Sophy," he said, "is it safe for you?"

"Yes," she answered; "God has made it safe for me."

CHAPTER XVIII. SAVED

The gale off the Cape of Good Hope was weathered at last, and the vessel sailed into smoother seas. The bitterness of the cold was over, and only fresh invigorating breezes swept across the water. Nothing could have been more helpful toward Mr. Chantrey's recovery, except his new freedom from sorrow. His trouble had passed away like the storm. He could not but trust that the same strength which had been given to his wife in her hour of fiercest temptation would be still granted to her in ordinary trials, from which he could not always shield her. Sophy herself was full of hope. She felt her will, so long enslaved, regaining its former freedom, and her brain recovering its old clearness. The pleasures and duties of life had once more a charm for her. It was as though some madness and delusion had passed away, and she was once more in her right mind.

The voyage between Australia and New Zealand, taken in a crowded and comfortless steamer, was a severe testing time for her. It lasted for several days, and she could not be kept from the influence of the drinking customs of those on board. But she never quitted

Brought Home

the side either of her husband or Ann Holland. In New Zealand, where no one knew the story of her past life, except Mr. Warden, it was more easy to face the future, and to carry out the reformation begun in her. They were poor, far poorer than she had ever expected to be, and she had harder work than she had been accustomed to do; but such exertions were beneficial to her. Ann Holland, as a matter of course, lived with them in their little home, from which Mr. Chantrey was often absent while visiting the distant portions of his large parish, which extended over many miles. But Ann was not left to do all the drudgery of the household unaided. Sophy Chantrey would take her share in her every duty, and seldom sat down to sew or write unless Ann was ready to rest also. The old want of something to do could never revisit her; the old sense of loneliness could not come back. There was her boy to teach, and her simple, homely neighbors to associate with. The customs and conventionalities of English life had no force here, and she was free to act as she pleased. As the years passed by, David Chantrey lost forever a secret lurking dread lest his wife's sin should be only biding its time. He could go away in peace, and return home gladly, having almost forgotten the reason of his exchanging the pleasant rectory of Upton for the hard work of a colonial living.

From time to time letters reached them from Mrs. Bolton, complaining bitterly of the changes introduced by the new rector, whose customs and opinions constantly clashed with her own. She found herself put on one side, and quietly neglected in all questions concerning the parish; while her influence gradually died away. Again and again she urged her nephew to return to England, promising that she would make him her heir, and procure for him a living as valuable as the one he had resigned. She could not understand that to a man like David Chantrey the calm happy consciousness of days well spent, and the grateful remembrance of a terrible sorrow having been removed, were better than anything earth could give. The old pride he had once felt in his social position and personal popularity could never lift up its crest again. He had gone down to the Valley of Humiliation, and there, to his surprise, he found "that the air was pleasant, and that here a man shall be free from the noise and hurryings of this life, and shall not be let and hindered in his contemplation, as in other places he is apt to be." His laborious simple life suited him, and no entreaties or promises of Mrs. Bolton could recall him to England.

Eight tranquil years had passed by when Sophy Chantrey detected in her husband a degree of preoccupation and reticence that had long been unusual to him. For a few days he kept the secret; but at last, just as she began to feel she could bear his reserve no longer he spoke out.

Brought Home

"Sophy," he said, "I have had some letters from England."

"From Aunt Bolton?" she asked, with a faint undertone of vexation in her voice, for Mrs. Bolton's letters always revived bitter memories in her mind.

"No," he answered, holding out to her a large bulky packet; "they are from the bishop—our English bishop, you know—just a few lines; and from the Upton people. It seems that the living is about to be vacant again, for Seymour has had a very good one presented to him in the north; and the parishioners have petitioned the bishop, and petitioned me to accept the charge again. See, here are hundreds of signatures, and the churchwardens tell me every man and woman in the parish would have signed if there had been room. The bishop speaks very kindly about it, too, and they want my answer by the mail going out next week."

"And what will you say?" asked Sophy breathlessly.

"It is for you to say," he answered; "you must decide. Could you go back happily, Sophy? As for me, I never loved, or shall love, any place like Upton. I dream of it often. Yet I could not return to it at any great cost to you, be sure of that. You must answer the question. We have been very happy together here, all of us; and you and I have been truer Christians than perhaps we could ever have been if we had stayed at home. If you decide to settle here, I for one will never regret it."

"Would it be safe for me to go back?" she faltered.

"As safe for you as for me," he answered emphatically; "do not be afraid of that. A sin conquered and uprooted, as yours has been, is less likely to overcome us than some new temptation. I have no fear of that."

For the next few days Sophy Chantrey went through her daily work as in a dream. There were many things to weigh and consider, and her husband left her to herself, acting as if he had dismissed the subject altogether from his mind. For herself she shrank from returning among the people who had known her in her worst days, and whose curious suspicious eyes would be always watching her, and bringing to her mind sad recollections. She knew well that all her life long there would be the memory of her sin kept alive in the hearts of her husband's parishioners if he went back as rector of Upton.

Brought Home

Yet she could not resolve to banish him from the place he loved so well, and the people who were so eager to have him with them again as their pastor. There was nothing to be dreaded on account of his health, which was fully reestablished. There was her boy, too, who was growing old enough to require better teaching than they could secure for him in the colony. Ann Holland would be overjoyed to think of seeing Upton again, and to return to her old friends and townsfolk. No; they must not be doomed to continual exile for her sake. She must take up the cross that lay before her, from which she had so long escaped, and be willing to bear the penalty of her transgressions, learning that no sins, though forgiven, can be blotted out as far as their consequences are concerned—can never be, through endless years, as though they had never been.

"We must go home to Upton," she said to her husband the evening before the mail left for England. "I have considered everything, and we must go."

"Willingly, Sophy? Gladly?" he asked, looking keenly into her face, so changed from when he had seen it first. What lines there were upon it which ought not to have been there so early, he knew well. How different it was from the fair fresh face of his young wife when they first went home to Upton Rectory. Yet he loved her better now than then.

"Willingly, though not gladly yet," she answered; "but do not argue with me. Do not try to persuade me against my own decision. You all came out for my sake, and I am bent upon returning for yours. In time I shall be as glad that I returned as you are that you came out, though I am not glad now. I shall be a standing lesson to the people of Upton."

"But I do not wish my wife to be a lesson," he said fondly. Yet he could not urge her to alter her decision. The old home and the old church, which he had diligently tried to forget, thrust themselves as freshly and imperiously upon his memory as if he had left them but yesterday. He had not known how great his sacrifice had been when he had given them up in his misery. Ann Holland and his boy shared his delight, and before they sailed for home Sophy herself found that she could take very real pleasure in their new prospects.

Mrs. Bolton did not live to welcome them back to Upton. The last few years had been years of vexation and loneliness to her, and there had been no one to care for her and to help her to bear her troubles. She had been ailing for some time, and the trying changes of the spring hastened her death before her favorite nephew could reach England. The hired nurses who attended her through her last illness heard her often muttering to herself, as if her enfeebled brain was possessed by one idea, "If any will come after Me, let him deny himself, and take up his cross daily, and follow Me." The words haunted her, and once she said, in an awed voice and with a look of pain, "He that taketh not up his cross and followeth after Me, is not worthy of Me." "Not worthy of me!" she repeated, mournfully, "not worthy of me!"

The rector of Upton and his wife have dwelt among their own people again for some years. Though the story is still sometimes told of Mrs. Chantrey's sin, the life she leads among them is a better lesson than perhaps it could have been had she never fallen. They see in her one who has not merely been tempted, but who has conquered and escaped from the tyranny of a vice shamefully common among us. There is hope for the feeblest and the most degraded when they hear of her, or when they learn the story from her own lips. For if by the sorrowful confession she can help any one, she does not shrink from making it, with tears often, but with a profound thankfulness for the deliverance wrought out for her by those who made themselves "fellow–workers with God."

Ann Holland found her shop and pleasant kitchen transformed into a fashionable draper's establishment, with plate glass windows down to the pavement. But she did not need a home. David and Sophy Chantrey would not have parted from her if the old house had not been gone. A few of her old-fashioned goods she managed to gather together again, to furnish her own room at the rectory, and among them was the screen containing the newspaper records of events at Upton. One long column gives a high-flown description of the rector's return to his old parish, and Ann feels a glow of pleasant pride at seeing her own name there in print.

Printed in the United Kingdom
by Lightning Source UK Ltd.
102054UKS00001B/59